An Adventure in Faith

An Adventure in Faith

S. DILWORTH YOUNG

GRANDIN BOOK COMPANY   OREM, UTAH

ISBN 0-910523-11-8

Introduction

THIS STORY IS HISTORICAL FICTION. It is historical in its set-
ting. The battalion did march to California. It passed through Santa
Fe. The members did pray that Colonel Cooke would turn to the
West—and he gave that order. They were attacked by bulls on the
San Pedro and did raise a Liberty Pole in Los Angeles. There was a
man in the Battalion named Standage, and another named Cox
who was actually killed by Indians on the way home.

It is fiction in the account of the action. There never was a Jed
Colby in the Mormon Battalion. Even those events which are historical are enlarged as the author imagined they could have
happened, not necessarily as they did happen.

The story is written for boys. Its purpose is to demonstrate that
the greatest adventures are had by those who love the Lord.

S. Dilworth Young
Salt Lake City, Utah
22 October 1956

ONE

Shanghaied

THE WHALE OIL LAMP flickered in the murky gloom, giving uncertain light, and accentuating the prominent features of Captain Ebenezer Strong. If there was weakness or softness in the face, the flickering lamp did not reveal it. Brought into sharp relief by its grotesque light were the strong jaw, the prominent nose, the beetling eyebrows. A captain needed to be strong in the days of the clipper ships. Men became captains because of skill and power in handling men, men whose only notion of respect was fear of the captain's fist.

Cap'n Eb, as he was known up and down the London Docks, was an experienced sailor. Starting as a young boy in the cabin, he had stood his stint before the mast. Two trips around the Horn to Australia and the Caledonians, clinging to the yardarm of the top-gallant in the gales of the roaring forties, hammering his way with his fists to the respect of the men in the fo'c'sle,[1] had earned him a position as third mate. From this he had worked, fought, beaten, and learned his way to the captaincy of the brigantine, Wellington, nine hundred tons weight, home dock, London.

---

1. The fo'c'sle or forecastle is the room in the bow, or front of the ship, where the crew has its quarters. It was fitted with hard bunks along the walls in tiers of two, usually. A table and some rough benches were the only articles of furniture. Each man had a chest known as his sea chest, in which he kept his personal belongings. The chest often was his only seat.

Outside, the heavy March London fog concealed objects more than a dozen feet away. Inside, it added to the heavy darkness of the captain's cabin.

"We sail at high tide tomorrow morning," said the captain, addressing the third mate, a tall, lanky seaman, who was standing, cap in hand, just inside the door. "The crew is short two men. I want those men on board before we sail. Take the bos'n and get them."

"Aye, Cap'n," said the mate, "Shall we sign 'em on first, or wait until they recover?"

"Any way! sign 'em, shanghai 'em, get 'em—when they're at sea, they'll bloomin' well sign."

"Aye, Sir, we uns'll try."

"Try," bellowed the captain. His fist smote the table a resounding blow. "You'd best not fail," he roared.

Leaving the fishmonger's shop after his day's work, Jed Colby started for home. He had worked in the shop ever since his father "apprenticed" him out at the age of nine. Here, within sight of the ships which came and went every day, he had learned the ways of fishmongers and the way of sailors on shore leave. By now, age fifteen, he could cut and slice and fillet with the best of them. Every day the barrels of fresh fish would be hauled through the door into the monger's shop, and each night the packed fillets of cod and haddock were placed in boxes ready to be sent to the big hotels up town. Some went to far-away cities. There was a small trade with the coastwise sailors who often stopped to pass the time of day with the fishmonger himself.

Jed cut across the head of the London Company dock and headed into the deepening fog. Unable to see more than a few feet, he groped his way by the dim shadows of the buildings. Each shadow he read and translated into its proper place as he trudged along. Even though dim, the landmarks were familiar from long acquaintance in all kinds of weather.

He had been walking for ten minutes when he recognized the darker shadow of the alley leading to the warehouses of the American Shipping Company. Two figures loomed out of the darkness of the alley. They were close upon him before he saw them. Instinctively startled, he turned to run back the way he had come, but he was not fast enough. The men jumped forward; Jed felt a strong arm around his neck. Suddenly a great light flashed before his eyes, and he knew no more.

"Bly'me you knocked 'im out cold, bos'n. If you'd a hit 'im any harder you'd a kilt 'im," said the mate. "You tyke 'is feet an' I'll tyke 'is shoulders and let's get 'im aboard before 'e comes to."

Along the empty street and down the long dock, they hurried with their unconscious burden. Presently the hull of the Wellington loomed dimly through the fog. A dim ship's lantern hung near the sloping gangplank. Up the plank and across the deck they hurried with the unconscious boy. A rectangle of light struggled momentarily in the swirling mist and then disappeared as though defeated as the fo'c'sle door closed.

"Now into the bunk wi' 'im." They swung the boy into an empty bunk. To a seaman sitting at the table the mate said, "Watch 'im. If 'e comes to, just you tie 'im up. We uns 've got to get one more before high tide."

"Aye, I'll watch 'im," answered the seaman. He arose and came over to the bunk. "Yer muster guv 'im an awful clout. He won't wike up for a long time."

Ordinary noises have strange new meaning to one returning to consciousness. The sounds which penetrated the ears of Jed as his addled brain began to function added to the confusion he was struggling to banish. He became aware that his head was throbbing painfully. A strange shish-whisssh, which he couldn't place, repeated in slow rhythm. Heavy steps overhead accompanied muffled shouts, and Jed felt a distinct rocking motion. Suddenly his head cleared, and he realized what had happened. The sounds were

perfectly comprehensible now. He was on a ship. The swish-swish
was the noise of the ship meeting the swells of the sea. The steps
and shouts were the men on deck overhead working the ship.
There was no mistaking the motion of the bunk. That slow roll
could only be the movement of a ship at sea meeting the mood of
the water and the waves. Jed sat up. The door let in a patch of daylight to the dismal interior. Other bunks lined the walls. In some of
them Jed could see sleeping men and hear them, too, now that his
ears were alert to sounds. Two men dressed in seaman's togs were
sitting at the low table. One carved a block of wood into a model
of a ship, the other worked at a piece of sail with the sailor's palm[2]
and long thick needle.

"Where am I?" said Jed, addressing the woodcarver.

"Wal, now, if 'e ain't come alive, I thought as 'ow the clip ye
got with the belayin' pin was like to kill ye. I guess ye be tougher
than ye look. Mebbe ye'll do atterall. Ye say where are ye? That'll
be hard to say just now, but usin' the best judgment that a seaman
able-bodied has when his betters ain't about, I'd s'y ye are in the
good ship Wellington, six hours out of London, headed for America. An' now ye are able to use yer tongue, the cap'n wants to see
ye in the cabin."

With that, the seaman walked over to the boy, took him not
unkindly by the arm and helped him to his feet.

"Stady now, I'll help ye." Up the short ladder and out on to
the deck they went. The cold, bracing air served to clear Jed's head
and ease some of the ache. The fog had lifted. As far as Jed could
see was a tumbling roaring mass of water. Each wave towered
momentarily above the ship, threatening to engulf it but was foiled
each time as the bow rose easily and the ship slid over the comber.
Overhead the great sails bellied out in the brisk wind, their force

---

2. A sailor's palm was a hard piece of leather which served as a thimble and was
worn on the palm.

heeling the ship a little on its port side. Jed, with the assistance of the seaman, made his way across the sloping deck. The roll of the ship caused them to lurch as they made their way aft to the captain's cabin. The sailor knocked. At the sound of a gruff voice bidding them come in, he pushed the door open.

"Here's the boy, Cap'n," he announced, saluting.

The door closed, and Jed Colby looked into the strong, harsh face of Captain Ebenezer Strong.

"Well, boy, what's your name?"

"Jed Colby."

"Say 'sir' when you speak to me, boy. Don't forget that I am captain of this ship."

Anger loosened Jed's tongue.

"An' why did you shanghai me aboard this ship? Me with my mother and two brothers to help support. I don't know what they'll do with Father dead this past year. Ye'd best let me go back to 'em."

"Ye'd have a hard time gettin' back with nearly a day out to sea. Boy," he said not unkindly, "ye'll do well to sign articles and ship as a boy before the mast. I'll pay ye seaman's wages, and ye can give that to yer mother when ye get back. Then she'll be proud of her seafarin' son. I was a boy like you once, an' I ran away to sea. I'm not sorry, either. The sea is hard, but it's a good life. But yer on my ship, and ye'll stay on it for a long time so ye better do what yer told."

In the end Jed signed the ship's papers. There wasn't much else he could do. If Jed wanted to eat, Captain Strong had said he had to be a member of the ship's crew.

"Now," said the captain, as Jed completed the laborious matter of putting his name to the paper, "ye'll jump when spoken to, and ye'll salute when officers speak to ye. Step lively now and report to the second mate."

With misgivings Jed left the cabin and went in search of the second mate.

Days at sea were full of activity. Captains of sailing ships controlled rough men by keeping them so busy that they had no time to think of mischief. In addition, any captain was judged by the care that the ship received. The sails must be in good repair and have just the right set. The rigging must have no frayed parts to give way in a storm. The decks must be holystoned to unspotted smoothness. The brasswork must have polish until it reflected the ship's work in its shiny surface. The binnacle must be kept protected, and the rudder and its cables inspected daily and made sure of operation. In addition to these constant repair and upkeep jobs, the men worked the ship according to the wind and weather that nature saw fit to send.

The men swarmed up the rigging at the shout of the mate when wind changed. If the wind died, the ship was given more sail; if it freshened (blew harder) the sail had to be taken in, or the sail might blow away. The art of knowing just the amount of sail a ship could stand and make good mileage was the art which caused men to spend years before the mast as apprentices. Then too, each ship was different and could be worked only certain ways. Experienced seamen learned the danger signs and learned the tricks to keep the ship afloat and moving.

To this life Jed Colby was exposed. Across the broad reaches of the Atlantic the barkentine plowed her way, meeting storm and fair weather with good progress. She sailed well, and the ship's log showed a steady number of knots[3] reeled off at the end of each day.

Sailing ships were the life blood of the British Isles. Stop the ships, and she would die. The Wellington was one of the links of the far-flung chain of vessels which kept the food and raw material moving toward London, carrying in exchange the manufactured articles to supply the world. Her hold was filled with cases containing bolts of cloth hardware, implements, and items to add to

3. Nautical miles, about a thousand feet longer than our land miles.

the convenience of a new land. Bound for America, she would put into the ports of Mexico, Cuba, Brazil, and Argentina. Then after a year of wandering to pick up cargos of hides, lumber, and other New World products, she would slowly beat her way back to her home port. If Captain Eb Strong proved a good trader, the ship's owners would make money from the venture.

TWO

Shipwrecked

DARK AGAINST THE EASTERN SKY, the hurricane clouds glowed then darkened between flashes of lightning. The Gulf of Mexico spewed the wreckage of the Wellington upon the shore with each heave of the surging tide. Planks, boxes, crates, hatches, broken spars, each in its turn touched land, rested a moment, and then rolled higher on the beach by the next large comber.

The ship had taken a terrible beating in the storm. The wrenching of the eighty-mile wind, and the heaving of the mountainous seas had done their work, leaving the brig slowly settling from the water taken aboard through her spreading seams. The masts were gone, the hatches overboard, the boats broken and splintered. Finally she floundered a mile offshore—near, the captain thought, Galveston, Texas. The captain loaded the remaining lifeboat with biscuit and water, and with his instruments in the stern, and the crew at the oars, rigged a jury mast and set sail.

In his log for the day he wrote:

> Terrible storm, wind 80, hurricane. Opened ship—abandoned at point near Galveston, Texas Republic. Crew in lifeboat heading for Tampico. One broken arm Seaman Jones, cut scalp 2nd officer Briggs—lost at sea—Jed Colby, cabin boy.
>
> Colby was last seen clinging to the after hatch in the midst of the hurricane—probably washed overboard.

Then the captain, having accounted for his crew to the satisfaction of the laws of the sea, set his face and boat southwest and steered for Tampico.

Often as they crossed the Atlantic, Jed remembered the captain's statement that he must work or starve. He often thought it was work and starve. The food was musty, the water bad, and the officers brutal. Jed determined to leave the ship at the first opportunity.

The hurricane was that chance. Washed into the port scuppers from the hatch to which he'd been clinging, he managed to get to the main hatch doorway before the next wave buried the ship with its foaming weight. He hung on between decks until the storm abated, then hid in the forehold until the rising water forced him out in time to see the captain's boat disappear over the horizon to the south.

Jed was not a particularly brave boy, but his life on the docks had made him resourceful. His desire to survive was strong. Floating at some distance from the ship he spied a hatch. He thought, "If I can make that hatch, I'll have a good raft to get ashore." The shore was plainly visible in the late afternoon light. Watching his chance, he waited until a high swell nearly reached the ship's bulwark and dove into the ocean. A hard swim of fifteen minutes brought him to the hatch, and he pulled himself aboard. A broken piece of planking floated near. Jed retrieved it, and once more aboard the hatch began to paddle toward the distant breakers. The surf was heavy and strong. In a surprisingly short time Jed was in the thick of it. Then the raft capsized throwing him into the angry surf. Desperately he paddled to keep afloat to get air—to live. He caught a glimpse of the sand shore as a wave lifted him high. Then suddenly a blinding flash and merciful darkness came upon him.

Jed opened his eyes with a strong light shining into them. He groaned—sat up—lay down again. He gingerly felt a great bump on his head. Little by little the memory of the storm and his effort came back to him. He gained a little strength and looked around. Not far away was the quietly receding tide, while scattered about were various parts of the ship, and very near was the hatch—his raft. It must have been that which had struck him on the head. To the east the morning sun was just clearing the horizon; this was the strong light in his eyes. Why, he must have lain here all night, knocked out, dead to the world. He'd heard the captain say that "Galveston" and "Fort Brown" were on this coast, but where? And what lay between? Jed looked at the shoreline. A long line of windswept, forbidding pines hugged the sandy strip. There was no sign of human habitation—only the wind in the trees, a few bird calls from the thickets, and the ceaseless roar of the receding surf.

He knew he must eat, find shelter, find people like himself. Stories of the horrors of being captured by the red men came to his mind. The woods looked mysterious and sinister to him now. Finally he decided to walk anyhow. Rising to his feet he gradually gained strength and entered the forest. Interspersed among the trees were open glades of prairie grass, then trees again. Jed walked aimlessly for hours while the sun passed overhead and began to sink in the west. Tired and hungry, he needed to find help. He knew nothing of how to survive in this strange land. Then he came to a trail running north and south. Deer tracks dotted the trail along with some small tracks which resembled those left by cart horses on the muddy streets of London. These, he decided, must be pony tracks, and he figured they were going north. Ponies meant men, and he set out, encouraged, to overtake them. Walking was not easy, but he kept at it until darkness obscured the trail. Hungry and tired, he lay down under a tree and slept the sleep of utter exhaustion.

Men have gone into the wilderness ever since time was, to take adventure, meat, and raiment. At times the wilderness appeared to resent the intrusion, and nature has engulfed the puny aspirants for fame. But sometimes the wilderness is aloof and quiet. Neither she nor her children, be they man or beast, become aroused at the intrusion, but suffer the intruders to go their way. The eagle eye of the red man misses the track in the sand at the edge of the pool, or the hungry wolf does not catch the scent of the defenseless child—no one can say why it should be so, but it often happens. And so it was with Jed. Hungry, defenseless, lost, and only a boy, although a well-grown boy, he slept under a tree through the night. No wild animal disturbed his sleep; no savage band awakened him. The forest and the plain had swallowed him up and obliterated all signs of his presence.

In the morning Jed said aloud, "I must hurry down that trail and find the men who ride the ponies; I've got to eat." He rose to his feet and started walking northward, stumbling along with his head down, trying not be frightened, but knowing he couldn't go much farther without help. Finally he smelled smoke. Smoke meant people. People meant food. He was not long finding the fire. In a little glade off to one side, by a spring of cool water, were the embers of a fire still hot and smoldering. Near the fire on a flat stone was a pan full of meat still hot, its rich smell tantalizing his nostrils. Eagerly he picked up a chunk of meat and bit off a large piece, then another and another. Then he settled down to eat. A noise off to one side caused him to look up, and he found himself looking at a tall, lithe man with a long rifle under his arm and a quizzical smile on his face. "Are ye hongry now, boy?" he asked.

"Yes, sir."

"Who might ye be?"

"Jed Colby. Jedediah is my real name."

"And where might ye be from?"

"I came ashore two days ago in a storm from a ship. I'm from London. I haven't eaten or seen anyone since, until I came to this fire and this food."

"Wal now, help yourself. An' in that other pot ye'll find some bread, corn bread, mighty good if I did make it myself. Ever been in this country before? No? Don't know about Injuns or Mexicans? No. Don't know there's a war? Not a week ago the boys down by Brown's Fort drove off 5,000 Mexicans and whipped 'em plenty. That's what me and my partners are doing, carrying dispatches to General Kearny from General Zachary Taylor. We saw you top the rise back there a ways and allowed we'd find out your game before you could seek us out."

"You saw me top a rise? I didn't notice any rise."

"Likely not, but we noticed you. It's all right, Joe." From behind a log rose the forms of five other men, each with a rifle cocked and ready.

Then amid laughter at the scare Jed had caused, all fell to and enjoyed a good breakfast of meat and corn bread.

Jed soon learned that the men had left Galveston two days before and were heading up the coast to strike the trail to San Antonio before heading cross country for Santa Fe. Plainsmen they were and scouts—men of a breed never seen before by Jed— a peculiar breed, born and bred in a wide, wild country, and having the rocks and hills, trees and flowers, birds and beasts, as their books. They knew how to tell by the shadow of the sun on the clouds what to expect from the storm. They knew instinctively the way of the north star in the same manner that a homing pigeon flies true to his loft, or a dog makes his way home over unfamiliar land.

Jed warmed to their joking chatter as they quickly cleaned up their camp. From somewhere one man drove in a band of mules to which were cinched queer-looking saddles—saddles with horns six inches across. Jed noticed too that the small feet of the mules were just right in size for the tracks he'd seen the day before and he properly decided that these were the animals which had made them. Although they looked to him a great deal like the donkeys he'd seen in London, they looked more trim, more shipshape, and larger. While he was busy looking at the mules, the men gathered in a little knot. The leader opened the subject on their minds.

"What's to be done with the boy?"

"Let's send him back to Galveston."

"Can't do that. Any band of Indians could pick him up."

"He'll be a nuisance on the trail."

"I don't think so. If what he's done is true, he's tough enough to stand it. I'll lay we can make a plainsman out of him. Let's take him. He can ride Betsy." There was agreement in the brief nods of approval. The leader called, "Say, you, Jed. Got any idea where ye are?"

"No."

"Know where ye want to go?"

"No, only I want to stay with you."

"Wal now, if'n you do that ye'll have plenty of hardship, plenty of tough goin', and ye might get rubbed out by Injuns. They'd like a scalp like yours to hang in the teepee."

"I have nowhere else to go, and I'd like to go with you if you'll take me."

"Sure we'll take ye to Santa Fe, and there you can get a wagon train goin' to the states. An' mebbe by then ye'll love the West so much ye'll want to be one o' them mountain men and go trappin' in the mountains for beaver pelts. They say the mountains are the only place, but I'd prefer the plains where you can see your neighbor before he lifts your scalp. My name is Skinner but call me Jim, and all these others ye'll know in time. They're good men who know the plains and can read sign. What's a sign? Ye'll learn soon enough. Joe, show this young 'un how to saddle a mule, and let's be movin' on."

Jed saddled a mule for the first time and was helped to mount the animal. He followed the cavalcade of horsemen and pack animals as best he could while they covered miles of forests, open glades, trails, hills, and watercourses. The first few days, he hurt in every joint and was glad when Jim would call a halt. Then the mules would be turned out to graze on the deep grass, and Jed could sink onto his back and just lie still. As the days grew into weeks, he became hardened to the work and began to enjoy the freedom of the open country. His ability to ride grew until it became a pleasure. And he quickly became skilled at saddling, packing, building fires, and cooking simple food. He learned the ways of men accustomed to hardship—men who paid no attention to fatigue, cold, wet, or storms. He saw the stoic faces of those who were injured but exhibited no pain, merely shrugged their shoulders and went on. No one could be left behind. No one could allow himself to be a burden either. He learned how to travel through a country. His rough companions were full of the lore of the trail, and their stories of close escapes and near deaths continually enthralled him. Every question reminded one or another of them of the time when—and he'd be off on a tale to curdle the blood. Jed grew to be adept at asking questions which elicited lessons on how to stay alive in a virgin country.

A dark cloud in the west reminded old Joe of the time when a big storm stampeded the stock. "Biggest storm I ever did see. Came along like a funnel and yanked trees higher in the air than old grandpa's shirt." Just how high grandpa's shirt hung never was clear to Jed, but that didn't matter. "An' the hailstones which fell that day were big as silver dollars, yes, bigger. They'd knock a man out. Just peeled the leaves off the trees, and it didn't take the stock long to hightail out of the country. Never did find some of the steers—what happened to them. Likely Injuns got 'em."

"Is a storm the only thing that can stampede the stock?" Jed would ask.

"No, Injuns are the most regular at it. They get pretty cute, too. They'll crawl in among the horses and oxen and cut all the tie ropes, then they'll jump up, yell, and wave a blanket, and the stock disappears over the hill."

"How do you keep them from doing it?"

"Easy when you know how. First place have mules. They can smell an Injun farther than an eagle can see, and they don't like 'em. Then don't turn all the men out to guard, just one, and he lies down flat on the ground right among the animals, and he's quiet. Then he can see against the sky anything which comes crawling up, and before they can do any damage, old Betsy cracks loose and there's an Injun scalp hanging on the belt. That's the way the plainsmen watch, and it works every time. Those army men never would do it, an' lost lots of horses." Jed decided he'd remember that system when it came his turn to guard.

THREE

Meeting with Indians

THE LITTLE CAVALCADE bore steadily northwest under the Texas sun. Suddenly Skinner raised his hand for a halt.

"Big Indian trail—looks like Comanche, but Apaches are near, too."

There it was—the trail from the plains to Mexico stretching off to the south. There were twenty-four deep-cut ruts in the trail made by countless generations of horses pulling travois. The trail was broad and deep, and nearly a quarter of a mile wide. What they were noticing now were tracks freshly made. At any moment they might be attacked. Skinner gave a few brief instructions. Mules were tied four abreast, with a man handling each group. There must be no stringing out; all must ride bunched as close as possible. But no one must fire till told to do so. They might go through without discovery, but he didn't think so. And then before more could be said, over the hill rode the Indians.

There were about a hundred in the party, all brandishing their bows and arrows and making great threats but keeping out of gunshot range. A chief rode out a distance toward the plainsmen and asked in Spanish for a parley. Skinner walked toward him and talked with him in Spanish.

"Where are you going?" asked the chief.

"We are going to Santa Fe to meet the white chief. Why are you stopping us? We are Americans, not Mexicans. We represent the Great White Father and want to be peaceful."

"I don't want to fight the Americans. Cigarito[4] is a good chief and likes Americans. You give me a paper saying I am friendly to Americans."

Skinner was relieved when he heard the Indian introduce himself, for he knew the friendly Apache, Cigarito, by reputation.

"My young men want to fight. Gomez want to fight!"

"Is Gomez in your band?"

"Gomez is over there," pointing to one of the most active of the Indians, riding back and forth, yelling, and brandishing his bow in the air.

It was apparent that Gomez had a stronger will than Cigarito could cope with, for suddenly he put his horse to a gallop and, followed by a large band, rode toward them menacingly.

The little band of white men quickly moved up a small hill where they could command its top, leaving Skinner talking to Cigarito. Holding their mules tight they faced in all directions, their guns ready.

"Only three fire at a time," commanded Joe, "and only when Skinner says to."

The Indians surrounded them but did not come within rifle shot. They milled up close to Skinner, and Gomez taunted him.

"We are going to rub you out."

Skinner told him to go ahead, but if he did Cigarito would go, too. And he aimed his pistol at Cigarito's head.

It was a tense moment. Finally Cigarito's counsel prevailed, and Gomez withdrew his band some distance away.

Cigarito, no sign of emotion at his near approach to death, addressed Skinner.

4. Cigarito befriended the early white men in this western area.

"You come camp near my village. I keep Gomez from fighting you tonight. Tomorrow you go. I keep Gomez tomorrow. After that you go fast—he not catch you."

There was nothing else to do. Riding a mile or two down the trail, they came to the Apache village. Houses were made by pushing the butts of willows into the ground in a circle and bending them and tying them together at the top. The outside included blankets, robes, or anything that would cover the willows.

They camped that night on a hillside within good gunshot of the village wickiup—if there was treachery, they could fire on the houses. No one slept; all sat in the dark, their guns ready.

The village was quiet all night except in the distant section where Gomez held sway. Here they could hear the beat of the war drum and the fighting cries of the men and women.

The next morning Cigarito said to Skinner, "I will take you to head spring—after that you go!"

"Sure we'll go, and thanks."

All day the cavalcade jogged northwest over the plains toward the distant mountains showing blue against the horizon, with Cigarito at the head. Riding at a respectful distance were fifty of Cigarito's band. Skinner told the men the strategy.

"We'll camp for the night at the spring. As soon as Cigarito goes, we'll pack up and get everything ready for a march and come dark we'll go dead north all night. Gomez will try and ambush us when the trail goes through these mountains some other way."

About three o'clock in the afternoon Cigarito called a halt.

"Spring ahead. We go back. Gomez watching, so go fast tomorrow." With that he turned and rode off with his men, his horses creating a great dust as they rode away.

"If Gomez didn't know where we were before, he certainly knows now," said Skinner watching the retreating Indians. "Sure enough, see there!" Even as he spoke a distant smoke ascended to heaven. "You'll see a lot of those in a few moments." They rode up to the spring which nestled in a little draw. "Jed, you watch from that high hill. Don't stand up, crawl up the hill, and lie down and stay down. If you see anything coming, just let out a yell."

Jed gulped. The hill was some distance off, and he felt it was too far away for comfort. But he'd have to be brave.

Up the hill he crawled. Soon he had a good view of the surrounding country.

"See anything?" yelled Skinner.

"I see three smokes."

"Where are they?"

"One east, one south, one southwest."

"Any north?"

"Not yet."

"Keep watching. They've probably got spies out on our trail, too. Gomez won't attack till he thinks he can do it without getting shot. Probably waiting for us in the pass, but wants to be sure we're going there."

"It looks like it now, but we aren't."

Jed kept a sharp lookout. The smoke reached lazily to the sky—first strong, then weak, then in puffs. Apparently the lookouts had some way of signaling the movements of the party.

Dark came; objects became indistinct. Jed came down from the hill and helped with the preparations. The fire was kept burning, but outside its light, experienced hands quickly saddled and packed the mules. Shortly all was ready.

"Put some wood on the fire," directed Skinner. "Make 'em think we're still here. Their spies will creep up close now; we want to be well on the way when they find us gone."

Wood was piled on the fire and then the men mounted and silently trotted north at a good fast pace. No words were spoken; just the sound of the creaking leather and the pounding of the hoofs on the plains broke the stillness. They had been riding about half an hour when Skinner laughed and said, "Look back."

Jed looked back. There on the high hill from which he'd kept watch a great fire blazed. He could see the forms of the Indians as they passed back and forth feeding it.

"Now they know we're gone and are signaling old Gomez. But they can't follow our trail in the dark, and by morning we'll be too far away."

All night they rode until Jed wasn't sure he could hold his seat in the saddle much longer. A great weariness engulfed him. Didn't these men ever tire? In the dark, he could see the six vague forms sitting, riding along, never speaking a word, silently bearing north. Daylight found them in a narrow valley surrounded by high hills, the forerunners of the mountain range.

"Two hours for breakfast and to rest the mules. Come with me, Jed." They climbed the high ridge.

Off to the south away against the southern horizon a single smoke column floated up, while off to the southwest, still farther away, an answering one hung dim and faint.

"I guess we gave 'em the slip, but we don't know. You sleep, boy, for two hours, and we'll call you when we're ready."

At the camp Jed lay down, his head on the saddle. The men were busy tending the mules, moving about; but Jed slept.

"The kid's kind o' tender yet," remarked Joe.

"He'll learn though, got good stuff in him," replied Skinner.

Skinner's party traveled by night for a week, then, seeing no signs of lurking or following Indians, they resumed their daytime travels. Jed gradually hardened to the rigors of trail life. He learned to conceal his fire. And, important for his chance for survival, he learned never to sleep near the fire. The evening meal finished, the men waited for dark, then moved off a mile or two before making their beds. A sharp nose could follow the smell of smoke right into camp but having found it could not trace the absent campers in the dark.

Skinner had learned, so had all the others. Any plainsman testi-
fied by his living presence that he had learned. Those who did
not, or were careless, didn't live to tell about it. Jed had the best
school in which to study—the school of hard experience—and
the best teachers, each one a living expert in the science of how to
stay alive.

One late afternoon as the sun edged toward the bluffs and
peaks of the surrounding ranges, the caravan came into a well-trav-
eled road. It was rough; it was dusty; but it was broad and had two
tracks. Skinner stopped and surveyed the surrounding landmarks.

"Santy Fe is north," he said pointing, "and it ain't far. Should
get there before dark."

The men laughed and shouted with anticipation.

"There'll be a fandango tonight," called out one.

"Watch out for the Taos lightnin'," was the response.

Even the mules seemed to catch the excitement for they broke
into a fast trot. An hour of fast riding, and they came into view of
the town.

Jed felt a wave of disappointment. There was a square—the
plaza, Skinner called it—and a long, low-roofed house with a long
porch. This was the governor's palace. A church was a short distance away. These, with a motley collection of mud adobe huts,
comprised the thriving town of Santa Fe, mecca of traders and
trappers, oldest town in the territory, and as Skinner pointed out, it
looked it. Squalid looking, and old as it was, the place was teeming
with activity. Skinner greeted half a dozen of his old acquaintances
as they rode along. Long conversations could wait. The mules had
to be corralled and fed.

"Well, boy, it looks like you've arrived," Skinner said kindly.
"I'll see if there's a train or scouting party going to the states.
They'll be glad to have you go along."

Camp was made; the mules in a mud-walled corral munched
their hay and grain; and the party was free for such entertainment

as the town could afford. Skinner's men made no bones about what they intended to do. They were going to a fandango, and they were going to get drunk. Wild men they were, and in the manner of wild men they celebrated their arrival.

Jed took no part in the celebration but returned early to his camp. Off to one side he noticed the evening fires of a camp of some nondescript men. He crossed the small creek bordering the canals and approached one of the fires. Shyly he stood back, not quite daring to enter the circle. A man noticed him.

"Hey there, boy, where'd you come from?"

"Come and join us. Have some stew."

A proffered bowl of steaming hot stew was handed him, and he was soon satisfying his hunger.

"What's your name?"

"Jed Colby."

"Where are you from?"

"My home is London, but I was shanghaied aboard a ship which later wrecked. I was washed ashore, and finally found Skinner and his men who brought me here. They said I could get to the states and then back home."

"My name is Standage, this man is Cox, and this one Hess; and the cook tonight is Hart. We're part of General Kearny's army, starting for California in the morning. All of us are Mormons. Have you ever heard of the Mormons?"

"No, I haven't," said Jed.

"We joined the battalion at Winter Quarters and have marched this far," Standage continued. "All of our people are moving west, and we aim to help them with our pay and some of our clothes."

"Are you going to stay in California? asked Jed.

"No. As soon as we're discharged there, we expect to go find our families in the Rocky Mountains."

"Where's that?" Jed asked.

"Out that way," Standage responded with a vague gesture that included the whole sweep of the northern horizon.

"Can I go with you?" Jed asked wistfully.

"Now, boy, you're too young to go off on a trip like this. You'd better get heading for either home or the states; that would be best for you."

The men went about their evening chores methodically and soon gathered about the fire. Jed wondered why they were not over to the fandango; plenty of the soldiers were, he'd noticed. But these men were different. They seemed content to talk of home, of the day's work, of the future—and before they went to bed they gathered briefly, and one said a prayer. He asked protection for them, for their families, and wisdom to do right. Jed warmed to this reminder of his own home and of the kindly minister who used to call.

As he left their campfire and went to his own bed in Skinner's camp, a half-formed idea was in his head. Why not go with these soldiers? They seemed kind. Tomorrow he'd survey the situation, and if there was a chance.... He drifted off into dreamless sleep.

Morning dawned, and with the dawning came the noises of the battalion on the move. Jed stirred, sat up, and looked about. In the distance he could see the cooking fires of the soldiers. He looked at his sleeping companions. Sometime in the night they had returned, but they were dead to the world now. Jed arose. Quietly he pulled on his boots and gathered his meager belongings. He was grateful to Skinner for what had been done for him, but there wasn't time now to thank anyone—besides, Skinner might stop him and make him go the States.

Jed skirted the Battalion camp. He passed the long line of mules and oxen, each having its last bit of feed. Stealing along the line he came to the parked wagons. Some looked loaded, ready to move; others waited for the addition of tents and blankets used by the camp.

Jed found one, which though loaded, had a space between the load and the cover. He crawled in, made himself as comfortable as he could, and waited.

"Hitch up!" rang out the command.

Mules and oxen were hitched to the wagons.

"Forward!" The bugles blew, the drivers cracked their whips, and the wagon train of the Mormon Battalion, California-bound, moved on to the road heading south.

All day the wagon jolted into chuckholes and out. All day the dust sifted up and around, enveloping men, animals, and wagons with powdery white clouds.

Jed, under the tarpaulin cover, was in misery from heat, dust, thirst, and hunger. Finally when he felt he could endure no more, the wagons stopped. Shouting drivers unhitched the animals, and the train made camp. Jed lay anxiously for an hour; then the smell of cooking meat came to his nostrils, and he could stand it no longer. Stiffly he crawled from his hiding place and stretched his cramped muscles. Then he sought the fire of his friends of the previous night. As he entered the circle of firelight, Standage looked at him with amazement.

"Where did you come from?"

"I rode here in a wagon."

"Well, I'll be—."

"Look," said Jed earnestly, "I want to go with you to California. I can help. I can do most as much as a man, and I'll work hard."

"Aw, let's take him," said Cox. "Besides, he can't go back alone."

"Let's go see the captain," said Standage. They went to Captain Davis's tent .

"Come in," said the captain in response to the knock on a tent pole.

Standage saluted. "Here is a stowaway who rode with us from Santa Fe. He hasn't any folks, and he wants to go with us. If he can go, I'll take care of him and glad to. How about it?"

Captain Davis considered. They couldn't send him back alone. They might have use for him—a good strong boy. The boy looked at him, a silent appeal in his eyes. The captain was touched. He listened to Jed's story.

"You can go with us," he finally said. "Standage, you see that he is given what he needs."

That night Jed snuggled into his blankets and dreamed of being shanghaied. But every time the brutal captain of the ship Wellington reached out for him, the form of Henry Standage foiled the effort. It was a happy dream.

FOUR

Joining the Mormon Battalion

THE EARLY MORNING MIST hung low in the valley of the Mimbres. The flame pushed back the darkness as Jed Colby added a large pile of juniper to the ashes of last night's fire. In the light he could see the low pitched tents of the Battalion. Jed flailed his arms across his chest to get warm while the fire took hold of the wood and gathered strength. He was glad to have his turn at fire building done. The night had been cold.

The men had huddled together in the tents, sharing their blankets, but even then their teeth had chattered most of the night. Jed awoke his tent mates.

"Come out, boys. Reveille has blown."

Stiff muscles slowly responded as men groaned their way to a standing position.

"Wow! It's cold," said Standage.

"Look," said Jed, as he held out the water bucket, "Watch this magic." He held the bucket upside down.

"Bucket upside down, but water comes not forth," Standage grunted. "It couldn't if it's as frozen as I am. How thick is the ice?"

Jed broke the layer on the bucket with the hatchet.

"Looks to be about a half inch."

"No wonder I was cold."

They helped each other wash—one holding the bucket while the other soused his face and hands.

"It's still cold," said Standage. "You've got ice in your hair." Jed accepted the statement without argument.

"What's for breakfast?" Jed asked.

"Don't know," said Standage.

Jed's stomach tuned a little as he thought of the prospect. Standage began rummaging around in the grub box. "I've found half a cup of flour. Well, boys," he said with a wry smile, "I reckon we'll be eating flour soup and lower tripe."

"I'm so hungry I could eat anything," said Cox, "so hurry with the cookin' and a little less of the gab."

Standage ran the pork rind around the inside of the skillet, then filled it about half full of intestines.

"Are they clean?" asked Cox.

"Thinkin' of breakfast this morning, I washed 'em in yon creek last night," Standage replied. Then into the boiling pot of water he carefully stirred the half cup of flour. It barely changed the color of the water. With his knife, he stirred the sizzling meat in the frying pan.

"Breakfast's ready," he announced.

In the dimly growing light and huddled about the fire, each member of the squad received a portion of the contents of the pan, and a cup full of gruel.

Cox cut off a section of gut and stowed it in his mouth. After chewing for a few moments, he announced, "Not quite as tough as the meat last night, but more slippery. If'n I could just get it between my teeth and hold it there, I might make a dent. You know, this is a great discovery. I've been wanting something to chew on while walking to California, and here I finally have it. This piece will last—," he suddenly gulped, "no, it won't. It slipped down." He grimaced at the others. "Well, what's the matter. If you're goin' to pull wagons you're goin' to eat." Each man tentatively took a bite. Pangs of hunger—desperate hunger—forced Jed to try a little of it. It was a little rubbery, he reflected, but not bad tasting. After eating the plate full and drinking the thin, watery gruel, he felt better. "Meat's meat," Charboneau had said. Charboneau was right as he was so often right. In fact, Colonel Cooke had employed Charboneau as the leader of the guides. Guts give a man guts to pull at the wagon ropes.

After the scanty breakfast the call of the bugle came echoing through the camp. Lieutenant Pace called out an order, "Hitch up."

"You'd think the colonel would wait until daylight," said Cox as he assisted Jed with the stiff straps on the mules' collars. "You can be glad you're not driving the oxen. They're pretty ornery on cold mornings."

"They haven't enough strength to be ornery now. This is a great system," observed Standage further. "You hitch up the ox and make hem pull your wagon. Just as he is about to die of fatigue you quickly cut his throat, so he can't die a natural death, and then you have shoe-leather steak and tough stew until nothing is left but the horns. Tomorrow I'm going to try rawhide soup. They tell me it's right nourishin'."

The bugle blew "forward." Each wagon moved off, two mules on the tongue, with four men pulling on each side on ropes attached to the axles and rigged to their shoulders with loops in the ropes.

Noon came after an eternity of dust, dirt, aching shoulders, legs long since grown numb. The wagons stopped.

"It'll be a dry camp," muttered Standage, "an' me not even able to spit cotton."

The exhausted Battalion flung itself into the shade of bushes, wagon boxes, anything offering relief from the sun. The heat arose in waves as the bright sunlight bored into the desert. It was fully an hour before the members of the squad could muster strength to prepare their crude meal after the day's ration had been issued.

Colonel Cooke was worried. He had heard nothing from his guides for twenty-four hours. His mules and oxen, poor to begin with, were fast becoming walking skeletons. He might be able to pioneer a road to the Pacific if he had strong, fat mules and enough food, but starting out with seventy days' rations and a ninety-day or more journey was asking too much. He sent his orderly for Lieutenant Smith.

"Lieutenant, how many rations are left?"

"Forty-three days of flour and sixty days of pork, if you figure short ration, sir," said the lieutenant.

"Hmm … reduce the ration to one-half cup of flour per day per man and one-half pound meat until further orders."

"The men are weak, sir," said Smith. "Further reduction will not help them gain strength."

"And neither will starvation," snapped the colonel. "Half rations are better than quarter, and quarter are better than none. Send a squad back on the trail and have them slaughter that ox we left this morning. That will help some."

"Yes, sir," confirmed the lieutenant.

"And then have a smoke raised. Perhaps we can persuade some of the Apaches to come in and trade. They ought to have some mules—they get enough from the Mexicans."

A loud call from the corporal of the guard brought a report of a dust coming rapidly in their direction from the southwest. In a few moments Charboneau and his guides rode into the camp. The colonel waited impatiently for his report.

"I find no water except small hole ten-twelve mile. Ride twenty mile farther, no water. Go five or six mile, find road go off southeast. Think it road to Janos but not sure."

"Can we make it southwest?"

"Depend on water," said Charboneau. "If can't find, can't get through."

In the meantime, a smoke was raised in the still air as men smudged a fire with some green grama grass. Straight and tall into the sky rose the gray-blue column—the ancient call to the inhabitants of the great mesas of the Southwest to come to a council.

"Do you suppose they'll see it?" Jed was full of curious wonder.

"Aye," said Standage, "they'll see it, and if we were a smaller party, they'd have us all scalped by morning. Just a few mornings ago I was up on lead tramping out a path for the wagons when I noticed some bushes or trees off on a bluff. I pointed them out to Carboneau and asked him what they were. He took one look and said, 'Those not bushes, they Apaches.' And sure enough, they were. The clever devils had tied bushes to their backs so that when they stood still they looked just like young trees."

The shrill notes of the bugles blowing officers' call echoed down through the camp at the noon halt, the bugler of each company repeating it. The colonel's voice was grave as he addressed the assembled officers and explained the Battalion's predicament:

"I am informed by the guides that they cannot find water for at least twenty miles beyond the water hole where we stop tonight. Charboneau and Leroux reported to me this morning that the trail taken by General Kearny is impracticable for wagons. These men say that by following down the old road which is about twelve miles ahead, which they think leads to the Sonora settlement, we can turn down the Salt River and strike the Gila at the Pima villages. It will take longer but will be more sure and safer. None of them know the country or where water holes can be found. What do you gentlemen think—Lieutenant Smith?"

"I think in our present condition we'd better be within call of settlements where we can get food and mules. The battalion is weak—the men and animals tired. They'd never make it going west."

"I concur with Lieutenant Smith's views," said Stoneman. "We should travel south. The road will lead past water, and we can have some of the comforts of civilization en route."

"My opinion is not worth much from a military viewpoint," said Captain Hunt, "but this battalion enlisted to go to California; we don't care much how we get there; and we are willing to endure hardships. We do not believe that to go south is our way. We should turn west at the earliest opportunity and strike out for California by the most direct feasible route. I think I speak the feelings of my brother officers and of all the men of the battalion."

Colonel Cooke dismissed all officers but Lieutenants Stoneman and Smith, with whom he held a long and serious conversation. The captains returned to their companies to report. Most members of Company E echoed the feelings of Captain Hunt, and worried lest the two lieutenants would influence the colonel to keep on south.

"I'm afraid," summed up Standage sincerely, "that we'll get into Mexico and get caught by the army of the Center, and then we'll get discharged in Mexico instead of California." Most of the men feared the same thing, and all during the hot afternoon, as the men pulled on the ropes, they expressed their uneasiness.

That evening, while mess was being prepared, two of the men from another company called Standage aside and spoke to him in low tones. He nodded.

Jed wondered what was so important that it would need to be whispered. Standage returned to the fire and told his mates that the men had overheard the lieutenants pleading with the colonel and strongly advising him to go south and strike the Sonora settlements. The colonel appeared to be wavering in his decision.

"Brother Levi Hancock and Father Pettigrew want us to pray tonight that the Lord will change the colonel's mind and that he'll turn toward California. Will all of you make that a matter of prayer before you retire?" All agreed.

Jed Colby couldn't quite understand such reasoning. His experience of the past month had taught him that strong men bent events to their own will. He had been the victim of men who took every advantage of every event for good or evil. People had to jump to the will of men. Here a strong-willed, positive-minded colonel was in command, and Jed reasoned that he would do about as he pleased. But here was a new kind of man. These men believed that by a prayer the colonel might change his mind. It just couldn't be done. Kindly as the men were (and they had protected him and shared with him all they had), they couldn't quite do that. Jed had had some experience as a small boy—when at this mother's knee he had said his prayers, and he had attended church where the pastor had called for blessings, but these had not been definite requests. These men were going to pray for a certain thing just as he as a boy asked for a pony. He couldn't swallow such an idea. Of course, he had listened many nights and mornings as these men had asked God for protection on their families so far away, but the men couldn't know how much, if any, of these prayers did any good.

These thoughts—serious for a boy—filled his mind as he did his share of the evening chores. Tents pitched with muskets as tent poles, wood for morning fires gathered, and mess dishes washed—then his time was his own. During the work Cox and Standage had gone off somewhere, so he was left to his own resources. Since he didn't want to go to bed alone, he thought he'd take a walk. The stars shone clear through the dry New Mexico air and seemed strangely close and familiar. He was walking on a road. It seemed good for a change to feel the old ruts, the hard-packed earth where the feet of countless oxen had beat it down. Some said the road led toward Janos. Janos might not be much, but it meant people and settlements. Off to the left the dim outline of a peak stood out higher than the surrounding ridges. Jed thought he'd like to climb it. He'd be able to see a lot of country from there, he allowed.

The faint cry of a wolf and the yapping of a nearer coyote gave him a sense of loneliness. He thought of his mother—what was she thinking? Wouldn't she be surprised if she could see him now? He turned past a point of rock and suddenly stopped. He heard voices. Instinctively he crouched close to the ground while he analyzed the sound. With relief he caught an occasional word in English. It wasn't Indians then—he could risk an investigation. Throwing himself flat, he crawled and wiggled through the scattered cover until he was just behind a bush on the edge of a small clearing.

Kneeling in a compact group were about fifteen of the battalion men. He recognized Standage and Cox and several others of the company. Kneeling in the center of the circle was the man called Father Pettigrew. Pettigrew was praying.

"And now, Father, we have come into this wilderness at the word of thy prophet that all would be well. We were instructed to go to California to help thy people to find a new home in the mountains. Our leaders now want to change our course and go to Sonora. Father, wilt thou change the mind of Colonel Cooke? We acknowledge him as the leader. Influence his mind and cause him to go to California as thy prophet directed. And this we ask in the name of thy Son, Jesus Christ. Amen."

Another man took the place of Pettigrew and made a like prayer. Jed cautiously crawled away. When out of earshot he arose and headed toward camp, feeling as if he's been spying. If the men wanted to pray, that was their business, but it sounded odd that grown men would do the things that only children did. He reached camp and stirred up the fire. Then he crawled into his blanket.

Morning came. The cold had penetrated to the marrow of all the men, so that as they arose misery showed in every face. Jed hugged the fire, but when the dishes were being washed, he asked, "Standage, who is your prophet?"

"What makes you ask that question?" countered Standage.

"I was just wondering."

The road to Janos, dim, but still a road, bore off to the southwest. The battalion moved slowly along its dim outline as the morning sun began to warm them and thaw out their cold, stiffened muscles. They topped a hill and looked down a valley. Off to the right a broad flat mesa led to a mountain ten or fifteen miles away and then disappeared around its southern end in mirages of cool mist and water. The road went down into the valley then bore off southeast toward Mexico—toward Janos—toward the Army of the Center. Colonel Cooke surveyed the outlook.

"Blow a halt," he ordered the bugler.

Glad for a breather, the men quickly sat down, while the panting mules stood with widespread legs, their sides heaving.

Mixed emotion showed on the colonel's face. He was a soldier. General Kearny had said to follow him down the Gila. The guides had said it was impossible but that around yonder mountain a way might be found if they could get water. In the one direction might lie death from thirst. In the other direction, the road was more certain—but it might lead them to a Mexican campaign. Suddenly his face cleared. Determination showed in his demeanor as he said to his officers, "I was not ordered to Mexico. I was ordered to California, and I'm going to take this battalion there or die in the attempt. Bugler, blow to the right. Forward, march!"

The first wagon swung off the road and headed west across the mesa. Unbelieving eyes saw it start. Then a mighty shout went up. Men sprang to their feet and, cheering and laughing, pulled on the ropes with a will. California—that's where they were going!

"God bless the colonel," said Pettigrew.

"Amen," echoed the straining men. Jed trudged in silence, wondering. Colonel Cooke watched them as they turned west. For a "give out" battalion they showed remarkable spirit. They might make it through, after all.

FIVE

Search for Water

WITHIN A MILE OF THE TURNOFF, and while the road to Janos was still within sight—and within easy reach—the battalion struck sand. The wagon wheels sank over the follies at each turn. The mules, able at first to go for half a mile without a halt, now could make scarcely one hundred yards. The men pulling on the ropes soon sweat out what little moisture was in their bodies and began to lag. They had not enough strength to pull. Colonel Cooke ordered a halt. This would never do. Some way had to be found to move faster.

"Why not tramp a road for the wagons?" suggested Captain Hunt. "Let the men walk in double file, just the distance of the wagon wheels apart. That should make the sand a little more firm."

"We'll try it," decided the colonel. "Half of the men will pull and half will break trail. Every hour the men will change positions. Give the order!"

The train moved forward once more, three hundred men breaking trail—tramping out a path—followed by the wagons—with men straining on the ropes on each side! They had covered three miles by the noon halt.

"Pretty slow goin'," remarked Standage as he flung himself down under a bush. "I could do with about ten gallons of water right now." His lips were cracked and swollen, and Jed could see that he really was suffering. His eyes were bloodshot and irritated.

"Do you think we'll find water?" asked Jed as he dropped down beside Standage. Since he was a boy, he was spared the rope pulling and had spent the morning tramping out the trail. "It's pretty hot, and I could do with some myself."

Conversation lagged. Too tired to eat, no one made any effort to get food ready. Each tried to rest as best he could and forget his dry throat that couldn't muster saliva enough to wet his parched lips.

Two hours later the torture started again. Each step was an effort—a result of the use of mighty will power which drove the men relentlessly toward the West. The mountain seemed still far away. As the sun sank behind its sharp crest and darkness descended, a worn-out battalion laid itself down to sleep.

Blankets were laid on the hot earth, and the meat and flour for the evening were issued. Each man ate his meat raw—sucking juice from the tough fiber of the newly slain ox. No one tried the flour. The mules were too tired to browse. The train bore the appearance, in the dim moonlight, of having been frozen in position, ready at any moment to spring up and move on.

Then, as though to mock the exhaustion and the suffering of the heat of the day, a chill swept down from the mountains and took the heat from their exhausted bodies faster than they could provide it. All of the night they lay shivering, covering themselves with their thin blankets, and trying to sleep. No, it was not exactly sleep, it was more a stupor that finally descended on them.

Toward morning Charboneau rode into camp. Has he found water? The colonel was anxious to know. Yes, there was water, but off to the right two or three miles—"A mere trickle," he said, "but might water the men." Then on the other side of the mountain and across the dry lake was a good spring. How far? A day—a day and a half—who could tell?

"We'll start now," said the colonel.

The bugle blew the reveille and assembly. The battalion staggered to its feet and automatons moved forward, guided by Charboneau toward the trickle—toward water!

Men dropped out and lay down, too exhausted to go farther. Their piteous cries for water haunted the ears of those who were still able to move forward.

The colonel ordered Carboneau and Jed to ride ahead and bring back water. Jed welcomed this assignment since he'd been spared the hard work on the march. He was keen to go with Charboneau, a mountain man, one who had known all the dangers of the trail. "The water trickled over some rocks and was lost in the sand," Charboneau told him. It was hard to find in the dark. What a country. He liked the north where a man could get to water often enough to be comfortable.

It was daylight when they found the spring. The wagons were still a mile away, and would take another hour, so they went about the business of filling the kegs. The spring trickled from an outcrop of rock and ran into crevices in such a manner that there was no place where one could dip even a cupful. It took the greater part of the morning to fill the two kegs. By this time the strongest of the men had arrived, and each tried in vain to get a drink by lying down, by filling cups. Finally, one man got out his spoon and filling that drop by drop from a trickle managed to take the edge off his thirst.

Colonel Cooke decided the only thing to do was to make it to the spring across the divide past the dry lake. So the order was given, and the tortuous struggle commenced once more.

Jed led his mule back over the trail. Whenever he'd come to a man down he would administer a cup of water. It was miraculous to see the speed with which a man, after one cup of water, could get to his feet and start going again. Jed walked all the way back to the last camp to be certain no one was left and then returned to the spring. The stragglers were there by now, using spoons and straws made from hollow-tubed desert plants. The straws proved best. A thimbleful of water would gather slowly in a hollow of rock only to be deftly sucked up through the straw. By noon the men were walking hopefully again.

Meanwhile, the battalion was having its difficulties. The animals, now twenty-four hours without water, were listless, and what little pulling they did served more to keep them from falling over than to draw the wagons. So the main burden fell on the men, already tired, most of whom had been able to get only a little water. Over and over, step after step, the men pulled, scarcely daring to look up at the distant horizon. Standage looked ready to stop and die right where he was. He couldn't talk. His tongue had long since swollen until it filled the hot dry cavity of his month. The sweat of thirty hours of desperate work mixed with the powdery dust of the march had caked on him until all that could be seen through the mask was a pair of tired, bloodshot eyes. There was no "give-up" in those eyes, but there was exhaustion, death. The train was slowly, inexorably reaching the stage where soon it would be frozen to the desert—its wagons immobile, its mules statues, its men held tight by the dead weight of two-ton wagons.

Somehow they reached the ridge skirting the mountain. As they topped its slope, a cooling breeze from the snowy summits struck them and partially revived their dulled minds. On the other slope the hill broke sharply for half a mile and then leveled off in a flat plain—the dry lake—and off across the plain they could see trees—a mirage? No, Charboneau had said there was a big spring of water.

Getting the wagons down the steep slope was hard, but the majority of the men found hidden reservoirs of strength. The wheels were "rough locked" to the beds. The men now reversed the ropes and "held back" on them. Before long all wagons were safely down and the dry bed of the lake stretched before them, level as a table and hard as stone.

The mules, scenting the distant water, suddenly came to life and pulled with a will. Colonel Cooke gave orders for the mule skinners to take the wagons on into camp. And freed of the galling job of pulling, most of the men easily walked the three miles to water.

Standage was tiring out fast.

"Maybe I can get there if I rest a while," he croaked in a whisper. "I'm going to lie down." Cox and two others sank down beside him. The afternoon wore on.

Standage dreamed that he was lying in water. He was soaking it up like a sponge. He didn't want to move … just make his bed in the water—let it cover him—absorb him—he flowed with water. When he opened his eyes, Jed was holding his head up, pouring swallows of water into his mouth. A star shining through the gathering dusk seemed to wink at him as he greedily gulped the precious liquid.

"It's a good thing I had a little in the kegs," remarked Jed. "That will put you where you ought to be." He gave a cup to each of the other men. "It isn't so far now," he coaxed gently, "I can see the light of the fires from here."

"I can make it," croaked Standage.

They arose to their feet, adjusted their packs and blankets, and shouldered their muskets.

"Better sing 'Jim along Joe,'" muttered Standage. "Old Doc Sanderson would judge us to be crow meat—let's march." Toward midnight they came within sound of the encampment. A spring gushed out of the edge of the lake, ran a short distance, and sank in the desert. Standage staggered over its bank, dropped his gun and blanket, and lay down in the middle of the stream. The water enclosed him—covered him—oozed into him. The blessed water—he drank and lived.

SIX

Trek to Mt. Guadalupe

THE BATTALION WAS RESTING at the springs of the dry lake after its two-day waterless march. Company E took advantage of the halt to make repairs in clothing, to wash, and to nurse itself back to marching efficiency.

A smoke made early in the day following their arrival did not bring any Apaches, but some Mexican traders ventured close to see who had made the smoke and were brought in by Charboneau. They couldn't tell the colonel much.

"This spring, it is by the dry lake Las Plagas. It is called the spring of Las Plagas, and the mountain to the right, that is the Our Lady of Guadalupe. It is the highest in the range. These mountains are called Sierra de Los Animos. From the distance they are, what you say in the English, animate, they shimmer in the heat."

"Can one see far from Guadalupe?"

"Si, señor. Very far. But it all look the same—great sierra—level mesas—on and on to the San Pedro River."

"Is there water?"

"Sí, but one must know where to find it. The Apachurraros de hueses—the Crushers of Bones? We see Red Sleeve two days ago and trade with him his men. Red Sleeve is very sly. He is afraid Americanos will kill his men so he watch from far off but will not come near. His village north from old San Bernardino Ranch—five, maybe six day away."

"Why is he afraid?"

"That is a long story, señores. But ten years ago a short distance from here an Americano name Johnson kill Don José, chief of the Apache, and many women and children at a fiesta held in his honor. Since then the Apache afraid of Americanos."

"Would you guide the command to the Apache village or to San Bernardino?"

"Sí, in two days we can return here and do this thing for five hundred pesos."

So a bargain was struck for guides.

That night around a great fire which warmed them in the chill November air, the squad sang old songs and told stories of the struggles of the Mormons in Missouri and Illinois. Jed listened to these tales of heartbreak and was deeply moved. His sense of justice was stirred. Surely the Mormons deserved better treatment than they had received, and now here were nearly five hundred of them in the wilderness to prove themselves loyal to their country. His reverie was interrupted by the appearance of Captain Davis who entered the circle and stood warming his back to the fire.

"Those traders finally told the story to the colonel why the Apache are afraid to come in and trade," he observed, "want to hear it?"

A chorus of assent urged him to repeat the story he had heard earlier in the day.

"About ten years ago the Apache scouts captured a young Mexican boy who told Don José, the chief, that the governor of Sonora had offered fifty dollars for the scalp of Don José, and ten dollars each for any other scalps of the Apaches. Don José did not believe this, for he was a friend of the governor and could not think him a traitor. He had the Mexican boy killed for the far-fetched story. A short time later two men, Johnson and Gleason, with a party of traders, came to Don José's village to trade. They said the governor of Sonora sent them to trade. They fixed a big pile of trade goods in the center of the village and in it concealed a swivel gun loaded to the muzzle with chains, balls, nails, anything that would kill. Then they invited the Indians to come in and trade and receive gifts. The squaws and children were dressed in their best finery and the men in their newest shirts. When all were gathered, Gleason invited Don José to go to the corral to see his fine mules. Arriving at the corral, Gleason shot Don José. The chief didn't fall but leaped on Gleason, bore him to the ground, and pulled his knife to kill him. Meanwhile Johnson had touched a lighted cigar to the swivel gun touch hole. It exploded and killed a large number of women and children and some men. Then Johnson rushed to the corral. Don José called him, told him that Gleason had tried to kill him, but that he was a friend of Johnson, and if Johnson would protect him from Gleason, he would let Gleason live. Johnson did not reply but rushed up and shot Don José, killing him. Johnson, Gleason, and their party then escaped on their mules. Though the surviving men pursued them and killed several, Johnson and Gleason were not caught, got away, and are still living in Sonora. The Apaches have sworn revenge on the Americans and will not come near to get caught again. They also have sworn eternal war on the governor of Sonora and his people.

"I can't say that I blame them for not coming around, can you?" concluded the captain.

"I don't think I'd care to be very far out in the desert alone if that's what happened," said Cox. "That accounts for all the signal fires we've seen at night on the peaks and the smokes in the daytime and not a sight of an Indian."

"The colonel is sending Leroux out with Weaver and is going to try to find Red Sleeve and bring him in to reestablish confidence. We need some fresh mules, and the Apaches have a large number they've stolen from the Sonorans. Leroux thinks he can bring him or one of his other chiefs in."

Jed sat, intently gazing into the fire during the recital. He did
not believe Americans could be capable of such treachery. And yet
here were two Americans who had done the deed—and within
five miles of where he was sitting. Many whites believed that the
only good Indians were dead Indians. Kit Carson, peer of all
mountain men, had said that you couldn't trust any Indian, but Jed
knew why now and sympathized with the Indians.

So wrapped up in his own thoughts was Jed that when he felt
a touch on his shoulder, the hair on the back of his neck rose
involuntarily as a wave of startled fear enveloped him. He turned
quickly, half ducking the expected blow. Charboneau stood grin-
ning down at him in the firelight.

"You boy, you one fine petit garcon. Tomorrow I climb
Mountain Guadalupe to spy out way and hunt for meat. I teach
you to hunt. You want to go, no?"

Jed gulped, "You mean me?"

"Oui, mon ami," said Charboneau, lapsing into French.

Did he want to go? Did a dry mule want to get to water?

"The colonel says you travel with me and learn to scout," said
Charboneau.

"When do we start?"

"Before daylight. I come and wake you. You want your musket—poudre, the shot—you can not shoot deer with words."

Jed's sleeping was fitful that night. The noise of the camp mag-
nified in his ears until every sound was an Indian attack. One
especially vivid dream he could not forget. He chased a great elk
he had wounded, and he almost caught up to it when it suddenly
changed into a bear—a grizzly bear which grabbed hold and
started to shake him. He suddenly awoke to find Charboneau
pulling him by the foot.

"Wake, mon garcon," he whispered. "It is time we move!"

To the mountain man of the Old West, the things done on a
hunt were automatic reflexes of things learned long ago—forgot-

ten by the mind, but unconsciously used by the body. And to the boy fortunate enough to watch one of these old hunters work, the whole adventure was one thrill of delight.

It was still night when the two left the camp. Charboneau, in moccasins, made hardly a sound as he walked, while Jed's every step was measured to the ears of the wary by the steady clop, clop of his boots. It wasn't long before they had reached the mountain. As they climbed, the sparse vegetation of the lower reaches was replaced with clumps of juniper and chaparral while mesquite was abundant and thorny. By the time they reached the first steep climb, the stars were fading, and the rich pink of the desert dawn was clouding the eastern sky.

They breasted the slope of a ridge. Nearly to the top, Charboneau stopped and motioned Jed to crouch down. Charboneau crawled up to the ridge and, choosing a small bush which grew on its summit, peered through its branches at the swale on the opposite side. He motioned Jed to him. Jed peered over in the same manner. He could see nothing but the outlines of bushes in the dim light. Nothing moved. For a long time they lay there looking, watching, listening. The morning breeze blew down the mountain, fanning their cheeks. A half sighed "aha" from Charboneau made Jed suddenly alert. Charboneau had the appearance of a hunting dog which had caught the scent of the game. He lay rigid with his nostrils distended as though to catch the scent, and his eyes were focused intently across the little swale. Finally Jed noticed that a bush had moved a little from the other bushes nearby. Then before his eyes what were bushes suddenly became bodies, and a thrill mounted his spine and ran up into his hair as he counted, not one, but three deer browsing quietly on the bushes not more than one hundred yards away.

Charboneau whispered instructions to the excited boy.

"We aim together. I grunt; we fire. I take the big one on left, you take one in center. Shoot behind shoulder and width of two hands high from belly line."

Jed aimed, but he couldn't hold the musket still; the gun barrel weaved in circles in spite of his efforts to place the sight in line with the deer.

"Now," grunted Charboneau.

The heavy explosion of his gun shattered the morning stillness and echoed and re-echoed from the rocks above. Jed shot, too, but it was a convulsive reflex from the noise of his companion's, and the deer at which he aimed drifted effortlessly over the next ridge. The big one had leaped high in the air at the explosion, and turning in the air, bounded away in great leaps. Jed rose to his feet, his face showing his disappointment. Charboneau pulled him down.

"Stay down, reload," he hissed. Jed obeyed. Charboneau had his gun reloaded and the patch tamped home before Jed had dropped another ball down the barrel.

"If you want to keep your hair, always keep gun loaded. If Apaches near, they hear shots and come running. Best be ready for 'em. Sometimes you think you killin' a deer, and you have bear charging from clump of brush. Now on that deer," explained the guide, "you too much excited. You must draw fine bead and hold steady, and remember not put in too much poudre or gun will give you what you call kick. Now let's go and dress buck."

"Didn't you miss, too?"

"This gun, she not miss, she shoot plumb center every time."

"But your deer ran away."

"Oui, he ran, but not far. Come, I show you."

They went to where the deer had been feeding. Charboneau pointed to a red splotch on a rock and then, like a hound on the trail, led Jed over the ridge beyond which they had seen the deer vanish. By what means Charboneau managed to keep on the trail Jed did not discover, but soon they came upon the buck lying on the edge of a rock slide. Charboneau cut the throat of the animal, and once more led out on the climb to the summit of the ridge of Guadalupe.

"What are you going to do with the deer?"

"Weaver is following us. He bring it in."

"How will he find it?"

"He will follow our trail."

Jed looked at the hard earth and rock formation of the mountain below them. If they had left any trail while crossing that country, he confessed he couldn't see it. Charboneau laughed.

"Ever'thing that moves leave trail. Some less, some more. Moccasins"—he pointed to his feet—"leave less than boots"—he pointed to Jed's foot gear. "Don't take much. Just like pattern. Eyes see land, all is as should be, yet in one spot small rock turned over or out of place or a bit of grama grass bruised. All has signs, and one who lives in mountains learns to read—or he lose his hair."

Jed made up his mind that he would learn to read signs, and he kept his eyes open to see anything that Charboneau would leave. It was discouraging, for the guide never left any signs that Jed could see. He asked about that and had another lesson.

"Good hunter or warrior not leave much sign. One can leave little trail if one choose. Indians in enemy land go for miles and not leave anything suspicious. These Apaches have been watching us for the past week, but we haven't seen them, have we? Every day their smokes have gone up on the peaks; every night their fires signal. They know how many we are, and they know our direction."

Jed glanced apprehensively around.

"Can they see us? Do they know we are here?"

"Don't know, they might have scout out, but I haven't seen sign. Keep eyes open and don't top ridge until you know what's on other side."

"But we crossed this ridge without looking," observed Jed.

"The deer ran up wind. If Apache there, they not have gone there. The deer show us 'safe' sign when they ran over ridge. That is end of lesson now, but do not forget."

He got to his feet and without further words led the way to the top of the mountain. The view from Guadalupe was awe-inspiring. A vast tableland stretched away in all directions broken by short spurs and ridges, cut and carved by the action of wind and storm into deep box canyons and gullies. Each storm-carved bastion was vividly colored with reds, whites, and lavenders. The morning sun gave the land the appearance of having been painted by a great artist who piled his brush with no order but for harmonious effect.

Almost at their feet was the camp of the Battalion, with the dry bed of Las Plagas stretching over the horizon to the south. Away off to the west a heavy ridge barred the way.

"How far away do you say it is?" questioned Charboneau.

"About thirty miles," hazarded Jed.

"It more than one hundred miles to ridge where San Pedro River and Gila come together. That's place we left General Kearny to come back and guide you. General Kearny told Cooke to bring the wagons through that way, but it is impossible. We shall have to find a way for the wagons this way." He pointed to the west. The prospect was not inviting. He could not see how anyone could find a path in that jumbled country.

"It is the water which we must find," laughed Charboneau. "Country always there; north always there," he pointed, "west always there, but water it never anywhere. The San Bernardino Rancho, it lies off there somewhere, we have to find Apache to guide us to it or Mexican trader, if he come back. Then San Pedro take us to Prima Village on the Gila."

The afternoon was wearing on when they began to descend. The upper portion of the mountain was a great jungle of great rocks thrown together in massive confusion, but it was solid to walk on. It was as if the Creator had started to construct a gigantic staircase to heaven and had tired and scattered the blocks. Here and there three or four giant boulders were heaved together in such a way as to make a cave underneath, while occasionally an outcropping rock would leave a cliff forty or fifty feet high to be skirted. One could easily have turned an ankle or broken a leg by being careless in descent. In the lower portion of this confusion of rocks they came upon a cavern-like mass.

Standing above it they tossed rocks into its interior until, nothing coming out, they assumed it to be empty. Charboneau crawled into the entrance between two big boulders and explored the hole. Jed crawled in after him.

"Grizzly bear he not home," whispered Carboneau. "Let's not be here when she come." And with that they scrambled out. They were barely in time. Clambering up over the rocks heading straight for the den was a large bear, followed by two half-grown cubs. She was immense, and almost white, the grizzly hair hanging long and grimy.

"Hurry!" yelled Charboneau, "up on the rock above." They clambered to a large boulder which jutted out over the den. The old bear caught their scent and rose up on her hind legs higher and higher until she stood nearly seven feet tall. Then the silence was broken by the heavy report of Charboneau's gun as he aimed at the white patch between the giant bear's front legs. A mighty roar escaped from the beast as she clawed and bit at the spot, then she turned and charged straight for them. "Shoot for her chest," yelled Charboneau as he hurriedly reloaded. Jed shot, but the bear kept on coming. She came on with the speed of a galloping horse. Charboneau struck the butt of his gun on the rock to settle the charge and rammed home the patch, barely in time too, for as he aimed a second time the great bear, with blood streaming from her mouth, pulled herself up over the edge of the rock. Charboneau emptied his gun into her raging mouth, not six feet away, dropped the gun, and drew his knife. There was no chance to run. The bear made one last effort to pull herself up over the boulder, then strength left her, and she tumbled back in front of her den in a great heap. The cubs quickly disappeared over the boulders toward the top of the mountain. Charboneau sheathed his knife and reloaded his musket.

"That was what you would call in the English a close shave," he grinned. Jed grinned back. He felt the color come back in his face, and he suddenly felt weak.

Charboneau tossed a rock onto the great hulk. There was no movement. He tried a larger one.

"It has been known to happen that bear come to life and kill hunter," he said briefly. After waiting half an hour he slowly approached the carcass, the gun ready. But his second shot had done its work. They stretched the bear out as well as they could. "She weigh 1,000 pound," guessed Charboneau. "Not bad day's hunting," he laughed. "One deer, one fat bear—meat's meat— your friends will eat tonight."

SEVEN

Battle of the Bulls

Jed rode with Charboneau across the desert toward the deserted mission of San Bernardino. For a second time he had been singled out to go with the guide on a scouting expedition. He was completely happy, and hummed a little song as he rode along watching the flopping of his mule's ears as he was carried forward at a gentle lope. Jed expressed himself a little surprised that the mule was so easy-riding.

Charboneau responded, "Best animal for riding is mule. He sure footed and not allow himself to get into places where no way out. He smell Indian center fire every time, and he warn you. He easy to ride, don't shake you up like a horse—important on long ride—and he can live on browse that would starve horse. If battalion wagons pulled by horses, we would still be over at Mimbres. Here another lesson. Don't ride along looking at mule's ears. Good scouts keep eyes open, keep looking all about country. Remember, I told you every place have pattern. Now while riding you notice if country looks normal. Note peculiar shaped trees—see if look different from one angle than from angle mile farther along. See how mountains lie, and how arroyos and ridges form. Especially watch the back track. Tenderfoot lose hair because forget to see lay of country. See how mountains look against sky. That only way you find your way at night. No night so dark one cannot see outline of ridges and peaks. Try to develop keen eyes. Indians are always practicing seeing things, specially things which ain't what they seem."

"Like the time that Standage told me about when he thought that some Apaches were trees?"

"That it. Those trees not in proportion—branches not long enough for trunks. They fool tenderfoot, but not Indian or mountain man. So if you see anything out of ordinary, tell me and try to see meaning of sign."

They rode for some time in silence, the creaking of the stirrup leathers, and the saddle trees, breaking the steady rhythm of the trotting mules. Jed tried to follow the advice of Charboneau, but the utter sameness of the desert landscape soon palled. Different trees? They all looked the same to him. He became drowsy. He had a deep sense of security, for he was sure that the guide was capable. He was rudely awakened.

"No! That not the way to be scout, to ride half asleep. Keep eyes open. You say to listless mind, 'Look sharp,' Indians are where you don't expect them. Keep awake. Watch. Now what do you see unusual?"

Jed looked but could see nothing that did not look usual. He noted three vultures circling high in the air. He noticed that the day was unusually warm, and he noticed that off about three miles was a "dust devil," a miniature desert whirlwind. "I can't see anything," he said.

"Don't you see tree with two trunks off there?" Charboneau pointed.

"Yes, I see that."

"No! but you will not learn fast. That is what we looking for. The second trunk is Apache. He hidden his horse behind bushes farther back. We go over there and talk to him. Colonel wants us find Red Sleeve's band. The scout may be member."

They turned off toward the tree in question. To Jed's amazement, the second "trunk" detached itself and ran across the desert toward some mesquite a short distance away. In a moment the Apache, astride his horse and thus fortified for flight, paused to watch the two. Charboneau signaled with his right hand to the Indian, but the Apache would not allow them to approach closer than a quarter of a mile. Charboneau signaled with his hand again. This time the Indian made a sign.

"He talk if I go up unarmed and on foot. You stay here and hold mules. I go talk to him."

"Won't he kill you?"

"I don't let him do that; he has no gun. I talk to him and discover where Red Sleeve is."

The guide dismounted, made a ceremony of handing Jed his gun, and walked slowly toward the mounted Indian. Jed watched, intent and alert. The Apache sat motionless on his pony watching Charboneau. When the guide was about fifty yards away, the Indian held up his hand. Then the conversation began. Neither man spoke, but each watched the other as the graceful universal language of the West created understanding.

"Who are you?" signed the Apache.

"I Charboneau, son of bird woman and Charboneau, the trader. I come from the rising sun to tell Red Sleeve that the white chief is his friend and wants to trade for mules. Where is Red Sleeve?"

"My Chief Red Sleeve is safe out of reach of the white man. He will not trade with the white Americans."

"The white Americans will punish Johnson for killing the Apaches with Don José if they can catch them, and will be friend to all Apaches. I talk with the straight tongue—I do not lie. Take us to Red Sleeve, and we shall prove our words with deeds."

"I will believe you—I will take you to Red Sleeve, but if you are deceiving me you shall die. Follow me but do not come near."

The Indian turned and rode away. Charboneau walked back to Jed and remounted. They followed the Indian as he jogged toward a distant mountain rising slowly from the plain. All afternoon they rode until toward evening they entered a narrow canyon which soon wandered into a natural amphitheater. As they rode in, the village dogs came snarling out. The yapping and snarling soon brought a crowd of Apache men from the crude dirt houses. Charboneau and Jed were quickly surrounded, arrows pointed at their breasts from all directions. A few had guns which were aimed at them, glittering eyes sighting along the barrels. Jed thought his time had come. Charboneau sat nonchalantly on his mule with no trace of uneasiness.

The guide was talking in a series of grunts to one of the Apaches who seemed more reserved and dignified than the rest. The dignified one nodded, and spoke to the warriors who lowered their weapons. Red Sleeve addressed Charboneau in Spanish.

"Who are you and what do you want?"

"I am Charboneau, the mountain man. My mother is bird woman of the Shoshone Tribe named Sacajawea. I am here to tell you that the great white captain wants you to meet him and trade for mules."

"And to kill our women and children."

"No, he will protect your women and your children against your enemies the Mexicans and the Navajos."

"I do not need protection against them. I need it against the American white man."

"The white chief offers the bond of friendship. He is great and powerful. He will give his word and keep it. He will give cloth, beads, axes, and knives in exchange for mules. As long as you will be his friend, he will be your friend."

So persuasively did the guide talk that Red Sleeve finally said, "I will meet your white chief in two days at the Ranch of San Bernardino. There we will trade mules. But if your chief have a forked tongue, we will kill you and all of them. You may sleep in the house of Red Sleeve tonight and tomorrow you may take the gift of Red Sleeve to your chief. I give you this belt of silver beads as a sign of friendship."

"And I give you my knife," said Carboneau, unstrapping his belt and presenting the knife and sheath to the chief.

"Tomorrow my white chief will give you blankets and axes."

From time immemorial men have feared the desert, for if one goes into the desert unprepared to meet its challenge, the desert will strike back and destroy him who trespasses on its sacred ground. If one fears anything, he usually hates it, and so men have come to hate the desert. One who lives within its endless monotony learns to live with it, and in learning to live with it, one learns to love it. Those who have lived in the desert a long time can find happiness nowhere else and are never satisfied until they can come back to the beauty of dry sands in moonlight, flaming sunsets, and immense distances. So it was with Jed. Youthful enough to stand the rigors of the trip better than most, he was slowly beginning to love the desert, and each day saw new horizons to enjoy and to conquer.

As they entered the San Pedro River bottoms Jed found new joy in pulling at the ropes, assisting the tired mules in making the extra mile necessary to reach their destination. The San Pedro bottoms were a mile wide at this place—a mass of cactus, mesquite, and manzanita. Following the bank of the river were groves of cottonwood. The river seemed to fight its way along, hurrying to keep from being eaten by the hungry sand and air.

Jed pulled on his rope, humming a little tune as he worked, digging his heels into the soft sand, keeping pace with Standage, who was having more difficulty and suffering more because he was not so young and vigorous as Jed.

"Standage, I wish I could let Mother know where I am. I am sure by now she has given me up for dead."

"All in good time," replied Standage. "We're heading for California where you can either board a ship or go back with us to our people."

"Where are your people?"

"I don't know exactly, but Brigham Young, our prophet, said that they were going to settle, he thought, in the Great Basin. They were seeking a place in the Rocky Mountains that he would know when he saw it for he has seen it in a vision."

"Our minister told us that prophets were long since dead. Why do you call him a prophet?"

"Because he is a prophet," Standage explained. "When a man is commanded of the Lord to prophesy to the people and to teach them the truth, he is a prophet, and Brigham Young is a prophet, and so was Joseph Smith before him. Joseph Smith was the first prophet of the new dispensation."

"What do you mean by 'dispensation'? I don't understand."

"Well, we believe that the Lord Jesus Christ and his Father in heaven divided the time of the earth into periods called dispensations; for example, from Adam to Noah was a dispensation. You know who Adam was, don't you?"

"My mother read to me out of the Bible that Adam was the first man, and wasn't Noah the man who built the ark?"

"That's right," said Standage. "We believe that the time of the earth is divided into seven dispensations and that we are living in the last dispensation. We believe that Jesus Christ the Lord prophesied that his own gospel would be taken from the earth. There would be nobody with the right and authority to teach the people. There would be no prophets, in other words, until the time of restoration. We now know that the time of restoration is here. Joseph Smith, our first prophet, was the man who restored the gospel of Jesus Christ in the last or seventh dispensation. The Millennium—you've heard of that, haven't you?"

"Yes, that's the time when the lion lies down with the lamb, according to the Bible."

"That's right. During the Millennium there will be peace on earth, and the Lord Jesus Christ will dwell with us. Isaiah, the prophet, said that in the last days 'the wisdom of their wise men shall perish and the understanding of their prudent men shall be hid,' therefore, the Lord will do a 'marvelous work and a wonder.' And he said further that the mountain of the Lord's house would be established at the top of the mountains and all nations would flow to it. I don't think anybody has imagined just how all of these prophecies would be fulfilled. Many people believe that they will be fulfilled, but no one has known just how. Joseph Smith found out how, and no one could ever have imagined that it would happen in just the way it did."

The wagons had stopped for a thirty-minute rest, and Standage and Jed were seeking what little shade there was under a mesquite brush.

"Tell me about it," said Jed.

"Joseph Smith was about two years younger than you are when a lot of ministers of churches came into the town where he lived in Palmyra, New York—that's in the eastern part of this country near the Atlantic Ocean. These ministers started to stir people up saying that they would not be saved if they did not confess Jesus Christ."

Jed questioned, "Isn't that right? I understand that if a person doesn't get baptized he won't be saved. My mother had me baptized when I was just a few days old. She told me about it."

"The ministers got Joseph Smith worried about whether he was going to receive salvation, and while he was pondering over it and wondering what to do, he had occasion to read in the Bible, and he came upon a verse. Wait a minute, and I'll go get my Bible out of my kit and read it to you."

Standage went to the wagon, reached into his pack, and dragged out a small well-worn copy of the Bible. He turned some pages and then began to read, "'If any of you lack wisdom, let him ask of God, that giveth to all men liberally, and upbraideth not; and it shall be given him. But let him ask in faith, nothing wavering, for he that wavereth is like a wave of the sea driven with the wind and tossed.' Lots of people have read that verse and thought nothing much of it, but Joseph was impressed beyond anybody's imagination. He felt that if he obeyed that scripture and asked the Lord, somehow the Lord would answer him and tell him if he should join a church, and if so, what church to belong to. He was a shy boy and didn't want to be caught praying by other people. So he went into the woods. When he made sure that nobody was within the sound of his voice, he knelt down and began to pray as he felt impressed by this scripture. A very great power of evil began to overpower him. All went black before him, and he struggled mightily, continuing to pray for deliverance, when suddenly he was released from the terrible power that was trying to destroy him, and he saw a light overhead descending. It was brighter than the sun."

"The sun's pretty bright," said Jed.

"Yes, it's bright, but this was brighter. Standing there in the light was our Heavenly Father and his son Jesus Christ—two great personages."

"Something's wrong there," said Jed. "I've heard our minister say many times that God is so big he can fill all space."

"That's why it was necessary for him to reveal himself to Joseph Smith so that when he restored his gospel for the last time it would not be restored on any error but would be restored on the basis of truth. The first great truth is that our Heavenly Father is a person, and we are like him, so he looks like a man, glorified and beautiful, but still like a man. And his son Jesus Christ is just like him in his express image—as the Bible says, in the express image of his person. Heavenly Father, so glorious as to defy anybody trying to describe him, looked at Joseph and turned and pointed to his own son and said, 'This is My Beloved Son. Hear Him,' and thus introduced into the world again the fact that he was a separate being from his own son.

"The Lord Jesus Christ asked Joseph Smith what he desired, and Joseph asked him what church he should join. The Savior told him to join no church, that all of them taught wrong doctrine, but if Joseph Smith would be faithful he would establish once more the true worship of the Lord. That was an answer to prayer, boy, and don't forget it!"

"Standage, back on the Mimbres River I overheard you and a group of your men praying that Colonel Cooke would be led to turn west and come to California instead of going to Mexico. Do you think that when he gave the command to turn west that that was an answer to your prayer?"

"I don't think it, I know it," said Standage. "That was a direct answer to our prayers. The Lord is watching over us and knows where he wants us to go. Brigham Young, the prophet of the Lord, has declared we are to go to California, and when the colonel was tempted to go another direction, our prayers inspired the answer. There is no doubt about that, lad."

The bugle blew attention, and then blew the "forward."

Once again Jed found himself harnessed to the rope and straining through the soft sand of the river bottom.

Occasionally as they passed along they saw at a distance small groups of wild cattle, some of which ran at their approach while others, more bold, held their ground, the bulls among them pawing the earth and challenging the wagon train to combat.

A mile or two farther they came out into a part of the bottom where the mesquite brush predominated. They passed through an open section where the brush grew back from the river perhaps 200 yards. On the edge of this brush there stood defiantly a dozen black bulls, their long horns lowered menacingly, pawing the earth and bellowing their defiance.

"I'm going to get my gun," said Standage. Those fellows might decide to charge." As though reading his thoughts, two of the bulls detached themselves with a bellow, and made straight for the wagon by which Standage and Jed were walking.

Standage yelled at Cox. "You take the left one, I'll take the right."

Each raised his musket. On came the bulls. Standage waited coolly, aiming until his bull was within thirty feet. He fired. The bull leaped and plunged to the earth, plowing a furrow almost to Standage's feet.

Cox fired also, but his bull did not stop. It crashed into the mule nearest him and lifted him high, throwing him against his companion, and neatly disemboweling the mule with his horns.

Standage re-loaded as fast as he could and fired a shot into the great brute, ending its destructive efforts.

"You must have missed him, Cox."

"I didn't miss him. He just kept coming. Let's put this mule out of his misery." With that Cox reloaded his gun and shot the luckless mule through the head.

Meanwhile others of the command were having their troubles with the bulls. One bull crashed into a wagon so hard that it tipped the wagon over and broke a wheel. One bull was shot by four different men and still did not fall but kept on charging. After half an hour of excited shooting, a dozen bulls had been killed, twenty more had run away through the mesquite, and the company stopped to survey the wreckage. Three mules were disemboweled. Captain Davis ordered the men to skin the bulls and take a sufficient amount of meat to last three days.

Cox cut out the heart of the bull that had been shot four times. Although there were four holes through the heart, that bull had kept charging.

"Lucky we weren't all killed," said Standage as he saw the evidence that bullets do not stop wild bulls.

Jed turned pale when he thought of what might have happened had the bull which charged him and Standage not fallen at Standage's first shot. Undoubtedly they would have been killed.

An anxious-looking man came running up to Standage. "Where is Brother Pettigrew?" He spoke quickly and hurriedly.

"He's over under that tree resting. Standage pointed him out. What's the trouble?"

"Don Johnson of squad five was gored by one of the bulls and is very weak. We want him to administer to him. You better come too, Standage."

Brother Pettigrew was quickly found. A few short words of explanation, and he was on his way to be the injured man, followed by Standage.

"Better come along, boy," said Standage to Jed. "This might explain some things to you."

They pushed through a small group of men standing around a man on a blanket on the ground. He was groaning and apparently in great pain. Brother Pettigrew knelt down by the injured man. "Are you hurt bad, Don?"

"I don't know," said the man weakly. "I don't think he got a horn in me, but he bruised me badly."

"Do you want us to administer to you?"

"Yes," said the injured man weakly.

"Do you believe that you can be healed?"

"I know that Jesus Christ can perform any miracle, and I have faith that he can heal me."

Pettigrew drew a small bottle from his pocket, uncorked it, and said to Standage, "You anoint him."

That night as camp was made, Jed was very much surprised to see this man walking around among his tent mates and assisting them in the camp chores.

"I thought he wouldn't be able to walk for a month."

"The Lord healed him," said Standage. "If you have enough faith, the elders of Israel by authority of their priesthood can lay hands on the sick, and they do recover if the Lord has not appointed them to death."

"That's right, Jed," said Cox, "I've seen it happen many times back with our people. In my own family both of my parents have been raised up from their sickbeds by the administration and authority of the elders."

EIGHT

Mission Accomplished

FINDING WATER was the Mormon Battalion's greatest problem as it forced its way through the forbidding lands of the American Southwest. With enough water, mules could pull wagons, men could walk, pull wagons, carry packs. Without it for longer than a day, the train became caricatures of slow motion gradually becoming immobile.

So it was that the week it took to go from the Maricopa Indian villages on the Gila to the junction of the Gila and the Colorado was comparatively pleasant. The days were warm, the nights cold. The sand, in spots, was deep, but ever, a mile or two away, the plentiful water—beautiful water, Standage said, was always there.

The Colorado River at the place of crossing was about half a mile wide. Most of this distance, by a careful following of sand bars, was not too deep. There was a stretch which was deep and had to be swum. Orders were given to make the wagon boxes watertight by using bull hides, and to ferry the supplies in these makeshift boats. The mules were to swim over. Captain Davis sent for Standage: "Standage, take some hides and make your wagon box watertight. Then you and your squad ferry the sheep. And don't stop till it's done—if it takes all day and all night."

Standage rounded up his men. Jed was assigned to keep the sheep in a bunch. There were twenty-six left of the original herd brought along for meat. Then Standage, Cox, and their men unloaded a wagon, lifted off the box, turned it over, and stretched the wet, raw bull-hides over the box.

"It'll leak some, I allow—," said Cox.

"We can bail it out fast enough to keep it floating," said Standage.

An hour or two later, the new boat was launched on the shallow water of the landing place.

"Hurrah!" yelled Cox, "Hardly any water came in!"

"Catch half the sheep, Jed, and put them in the wagon box."

Jed had a great time chasing down the sheep. One at a time he managed to catch a leg, throw the sheep, and then with legs tied, carry it to the makeshift boat. Soon the boat was full of sheep.

Meanwhile the men had fashioned two clumsy paddles from an extra plank carried for wagon repairs. One man was assigned to watch the sheep which were to be brought later, Cox and Standage were named the paddlers, and Jed was put in charge of steering the boat using a shovel for a rudder.

"Take the shovel and use it for a rudder to steer us," Jed was commanded.

With Standage and Cox vigorously paddling, and Jed doing his best to steer by the shovel at the rear, the box slowly crossed the river. It was tiring work, and by the time the first sheep were delivered and the return made, all were exhausted, and night was upon them.

A good supper of beans and bacon brought new strength. More sheep were loaded, and the craft started once more. The night made the work more difficult. Jed had to steer toward a fire on the opposite shore.

The wagon box was not steady in the water and had to be balanced by the men, and in the dark, no one noticed that the sheep were bunched on one side—the downstream side. Cox jumped to the side one time to help Standage swing the heavy box in line with the fire to which they were heading. His weight was too much; the box turned over on its side, throwing men and sheep into the icy water.

Jed was a fair swimmer, but for a moment or two he could not get his breath. He could not see anything to guide him, and in the confusion swam aimlessly. The cold water took his strength rapidly, and he despaired of ever reaching shore.

He thought of his mother and of his home. He'd never return now. He'd drown in the icy water. Then he remembered that Standage and Cox and all the others prayed when they were in trouble.

"Oh, Lord, help me out of this," he said aloud. "Thou helped them, help me!"

His thrashing had touched something hard. He reached almost automatically, and felt the round firmness of the makeshift paddle. Both hands closed on it, and with that extra support he found new strength and courage. After an eternity of effort, his feet touched bottom, and he pulled himself up on the shore—exhausted, wet, and cold. As he lay resting, he said aloud, "Now what would Charboneau do? How would he get out of a tight spot?"

He reasoned. "The river would carry me downstream a long distance. I don't know which bank I am on, but we were most of the way across, so I must have reached the west bank. Now if I find out which way the water flows and work in the opposite direction, I should be able to find the camp." He wondered too if Cox and Standage had drowned.

Finding a stick, in the darkness he waded out a short distance and launched it. Watching the stick float away, he knew the direction of the flow. He waded to shore and started walking in the opposite direction. After a time, the vigorous walk warming him a little, he turned a bend, and there, a quarter mile away, he could see the fires of the battalion.

Finding his own squad fire, he walked into the fire-lit circle and was greeted with joyous shouts. Quickly he removed his wet clothes, wrapped himself in a blanket, and lay near the fire. After he had rested. Standage questioned him.

"How did you manage to escape, lad?"

"I don't know," said Jed. "I felt like I couldn't last another moment, but I remembered that when you had trouble, you always prayed to God for help. So I prayed for help, and just as I finished praying, one of the oars touched my hand. I grabbed it, and with that much float I managed to get to shore."

"It's the hand of the Lord," replied Standage.

As Jed lay in the blanket getting snugly warm, he agreed with Standage. In that great hopeless dark only a miracle could have placed that oar where his hand could touch it.

After crossing the Colorado, the battalion had two weeks of terrible hardship. At one place passing through a mountain range, they had to take the first wagons apart to get them through a narrow crevice. Then they picked and blasted it wide enough to squeeze the remainder of the wagons through. Finally, hungry and worn, they reached the Pacific Ocean near San Diego Mission—a small mud-walled village. From there, they turned north and reported to General Kearny, at the mission and town of Los Angeles—not much larger than San Diego, but headquarters for the victorious Americans in their conquest of California.

For several days the men rested. Fresh beef was rationed to them. Colonel Cooke ordered that a large pole be raised—a liberty pole—from which the stars and stripes could be flown. Jed accompanied the squad as they searched the surrounding hills for an appropriate tree. Finally they found a slim tree stretching forty feet into the air. Down it came with a crash, as they vigorously applied the ax. A team of mules was hitched to one end; it was dragged to the place of the celebration and quickly raised, with a rope halyard attached to the top.

The battalion was assembled. A more nondescript, motley group of men could not have been found. They had little discipline of marching order, they didn't keep step, they were rugged and worn, and their clothing was in the last stages of repair.

Colonel Cooke, riding on his horse, his army uniform well-kept, well-brushed, was a sharp contrast to the ragged men under his command. He did not seem to notice their wretched appearance. With pride his eyes swept the ranks—each company drawn up into a semblance of order behind its captain. His lieutenants, as an escort to him, sat their horses easily. Their fresh-scrubbed, newly shaved faces shone, and their uniforms matched that of their leader.

To the notes of the bugle playing "To the Colors," the flag was raised on the liberty pole forty feet above the earth—high as a four-story building—its stars and stripes brilliant against the clear California sky.

The colonel cleared his throat. He read his last order: "The lieutenant colonel commanding congratulates the battalion on their safe arrival on the shore of the Pacific Ocean and the conclusion of their march of over two thousand miles.

"History may be searched in vain for an equal march of infantry. Half of it has been through a wilderness where nothing but savages and wild beasts are found, or deserts where, for want of water, there is no living creature. There, with almost hopeless labor we have dug deep wells, which the future traveler will enjoy. Without a guide who had traversed them, we have ventured into trackless tablelands where water was not found for several marches. With crowbar and pick and ax in hand, we have worked our way over mountains which seemed to defy aught save the wild goat and hewed a passage through a chasm of living rock more narrow than our wagons. To bring these first wagons to the Pacific, we have preserved the strength of our mules by herding them over large tracts, which you have laboriously guarded without loss. The garrison of the four presidios of Sonora concentrated with the walls of Tucson gave us no pause. We drove them out, with their artillery, but our intercourse with the citizens was unmarked by a single act of injustice. Thus, marching half-naked and half-fed, and living upon wild animals, we have discovered and made a road of great value to our country.

"Arrived at the first settlement of California, after a single day's rest, you cheerfully turned off from route to this point of promised repose, to enter upon a campaign, and meet, as we supposed, the approach of an enemy; and this too, without even salt to season your sole subsistence of fresh meat....

"Lieutenant Colonel P. St. George Cooke P.C. Merrill, Adjutant."

As he concluded the order, a mighty cheer came spontaneously from the assembled men; hats were thrown into the air; and for a moment all men gave vent to their happy emotions in resounding shouts.

"Three cheers for Colonel Cooke!" shouted someone.

"Hurrah! Hurrah! Hurrah!" The cheers were given with a will.

The colonel raised his hand; silence fell on the men.

"Men of the Battalion. This concludes your year of service, and you are now discharged from duty in the United States Army. However, the army still has need of you. If you will, I urge you to enlist for another year. We offer you good terms. These will be explained by Lieutenant Stoneman to those who are interested. There is much work to be done here to insure the stability of our government. There is good land, and at the end of the year you will be able to settle on your own farm, long before settlers from the States. You'll get the best land. Think it over; we need you!"

"Dismissed," shouted the adjutant.

The men walked back to their camp. Jed heard talk on all sides as men discussed the proposition of the colonel. Should they stay and establish themselves, or should they now find their families and cast their lot once more with the Saints?

For several days discussion went on as the men finally came to their decisions.

One afternoon Jed found Standage sitting on a log in front of his tent quietly repairing an old saddle. Long strips of rawhide, thoroughly wet, lay across the log as he carefully sewed together torn parts of leather to make the saddle usable. Cox was mending a holster. Jed sat and watched him. Standage finally spoke.

"We've agreed we aren't going to enlist in the Army. We're going home. There will be twenty others in our party. Each is quietly buying animals, for the minute we announce our need, the price will double or triple. I aim to use two of my horses for pack animals to carry bedding, the grub, and the tent. I'll ride the mule. There's still an extra horse, Jed; we'd like very much to have you join us if you'd like to. You can ride that extra horse."

"I bought two horses," said Cox, "one to ride and one to carry my pack."

"Before you decide," said Standage, "there are two other things you can do. You've proved you're a good workman, strong and able, so you could enlist in the army. Or you can go with us as far as Sacramento and then work your way down the river to San Francisco and eventually get a ship for home—that will be a long wait, in my opinion. Or you can go with us and meet our people in the Rocky Mountains. That's what we'd like you to do, if you care to do it. I bought this horse extra so in case you decided to go with us."

Jed was touched by Standage's concern. He thought of his mother and his home and his anxiety to see them once more.

"Do you think," he said, "that I might be able to get home if I go with you?"

"There is no doubt about it," replied Standage. "As the wagon trains of our people move west, there will be many groups going east on missions and to obtain supplies, and you can easily join one and get to the Missouri River. After that you can work your way to New York or Boston and take a ship home. Think it over, boy, and let me know."

As Jed thought of his home and his mother and brothers and sisters, a surge of homesickness swept over him. Why not go to San Francisco and take a ship for home immediately? He dwelt on this idea lovingly. He could see in his mind his mother's anxious face suddenly transfigured with joy as he entered the room without warning. She had probably given him up for dead by now. He would surprise her. Then he remembered his last difficulty with ships. These were very recent, harsh memories, and he could not quite bring himself yet to seek that method of travel to get home.

On the other hand, here were his friends—Standage, Cox, and other members of the battalion—with whom he had work-ed and slept and eaten. Each man was a close companion; each man treated him well and with respect. He would stay with Standage. Standage had offered him a horse on which to ride and provisions for the trip. He would go to the Rocky Mountains and see firsthand what these Mormons were like.

He sought Standage. "I've made up my mind," he said. "I think I'll go with you, and I'll do my best to help."

"You can be a great deal of help, and we'll all be glad to have you go. We'll have to arrange to get provisions and see that our horses are shod. We have to get packsaddles and pack equipment. We need enough blankets to keep us warm, and cooking utensils. I'll get you a good gun and buy a supply of lead and a mold to run the bul-lets and some powder so you can shoot and protect yourself."

The next two weeks were full of activity for Jed Colby. Under Standage's guidance, he was able to find a fairly good saddle on which to ride—Spanish style with a wide horn. He practiced packing the animals they were going to use until he could get all their material on the two animals Standage had purchased.

One morning in the spring, with the mocking birds singing in the oak trees, Standage gave the command to mount. Jed threw his leg across the saddle, gathered up the reins, and clucked to his horse. The little cavalcade moved off through the valley toward the north.

The men in the party were divided into groups and took turns leading the pack animals so they would not lag behind. Some men would cook the meals when they stopped; others would mount guard at night to keep the marauding Indians from disturbing them. By changing shifts each man had his share of all the work. Sometimes Jed rode along with Standage as he led the procession up the dim trails toward the mountains. Other times he rode with Cox at the rear and helped keep the horses from straying. At all times he was happy because there was a good deal of freedom allowed in their travel. Night and morning prayers were said. Each night after the cooking fires had been exhausted, the men moved the cavalcade on for a mile or two in the dark so that any Indians smelling the smoke of the campfires would find nobody there, and not be able to follow them in the dark.

Jed luxuriated in the joy of riding. After he had joined the battalion in Santa Fe it had often been his daily lot to pull wagons through sand, dust, and mud. Now he was riding a horse, temporarily his own, nobody to tell him when to get on and when to get off, having no wagons to drag. This was a grand new experience for Jed, and he made the most of it. His new friends had proved to be true friends. In their anxiety to take care of him, they saw that he suffered no want. And Jed was content to stay with them. He thought how different these men were from other men—both the sailors he had grown up with and the frontiersmen of Sante Fe and Los Angeles.

NINE

Jed's Decision

THESE MORMONS PRAYED. He remembered the time they had prayed to have the wagons turn west, and miraculously enough at the proper moment Colonel Cooke had ordered the wagons to the west. He remembered with gratitude how he had prayed when he was in the Colorado River with death threatening him, and how miraculously the heavy wooden oar had floated within his reach, how he had grasped it and with that additional help he had been able to work to shore. He had seen them praying around their campfires and asking the help of a being to whom they seemed to feel very close. He spurred his horse up beside Standage and abruptly opened the conversation. "Standage, why do they call you men Mormons?"

"Well, rightly," said Standage, "our name is not Mormons. Our true name is the Church of Jesus Christ of Latter-day Saints. But why are we called Mormons? I told you some time ago that Joseph Smith saw in a vision our Heavenly Father and his son, Jesus Christ. Four years after that occurred, one night there came to Joseph Smith in a vision an angel who said his name was Moroni. He said also that he had lived on the American continent and had been the record keeper or historian of an immense nation of people who had known Christ and that his father had written a history of these people. After a period of preparation lasting four years, Joseph Smith was given the plates that contain this history.

By the gift and power of Almighty God, Joseph dictated a translation of the writing on the plates to a man by the name of Oliver Cowdery, who became his chief assistant. When he finished dictating, Joseph discovered that the name of the book—containing a history of the ancient people who were before the Indians—was the Book of Mormon. The father of the angel was named Mormon, and he was the one who had made the record.

"Joseph Smith published the book, and after that when anybody believed and accepted the Book of Mormon and joined the Church of Jesus Christ of Latter-day Saints, people called them Mormons. So we are called Mormons, but it is only a nickname. Would you like to read the Book of Mormon?"

Jed was curious to see this book that had been given to the Mormons by an angel, and he promptly said yes.

"When I unload my pack tonight, I'll let you take my copy. I want to tell you, Jed, that it's a true story of the ancient American Indians, and if you will read it with a pure heart and ask God the Father to reveal to you its truth, he will show you it is true by his Holy Spirit. You will know it as you read it."

"Do the Mormons have the plates of the Book of Mormon?"

"No," replied Standage, "When Joseph finished translating the record, he gave the record back to the angel, Moroni, who told Joseph Smith that the time had come for the gospel to be restored and for the power of God to be manifested once more among men."

"Once more?" asked Jed. "Hasn't it always been manifested among men?"

"No," replied Standage, "it hasn't. Men have thought they had the true gospel, but they did not. There was a great apostatizing from the way of the Lord. About two hundred years after Christ's resurrection, nobody on earth had the authority to preach the gospel. But men claimed they had the right and preached what they thought was the gospel. Other men believed them, and so churches have kept going through the years."

"Well, how are they wrong?" said Jed.

"Let me illustrate just one thing. Have you ever read the Bible?" Jed said that he had, a little.

"Do you remember reading in Acts that the Savior was taken up; and a cloud received him out of their sight. And while they looked steadfastly toward heaven as he went up, behold two men stood by them in white apparel; which also said, 'Ye men of Galilee, why stand ye gazing up into heaven, this same Jesus, which is taken up from you into heaven, shall so come in like manner as ye have seen him go into heaven?'

"Now in spite of the very plain statement of that particular scripture, the churches today say that Jesus was a manifestation. That is, he was an earthly appearance of God who has no body and no form and dwells everywhere and has all power, and yet one can't see him or see what he is like. Jesus' body was resurrected, he went into heaven, and they saw his body ascend to heaven. Later on, men said that Christ and the Father are the same great force, but do not have any form. They have perverted the scriptures and have changed the everlasting doctrine. That is only one example, Jed; there are a great many. Let me give you another one."

"Let me think about this one for awhile, Standage, before you give me any more," said Jed. "This is a new thing for me. Ever since I was a small boy my mother has taught me that God and the Savior and the Holy Ghost are the same being and one person and that they fill the immensity of space and have no form.

"Quite awhile ago you told me that when your prophet— what's his name, Joseph Smith?—had a vision, he saw God the Father and his Son Jesus Christ, who were two persons in form like man. I didn't know what to think. Now you are telling me that all the churches have taught that particular thing wrong and that Joseph Smith corrected them. I want to know more about it, but I want to think about this."

They rode on in silence.

The afternoon wore on; the dust kicked up by the ponies' feet enveloped them in heavy clouds. The sun was sinking low in the west when Standage called a halt by a clear stream of water which flowed through a grove of immense oak trees. The surrounding territory was free of vegetation except for an occasional grove of trees.

"We'll stop until dark," said Standage. "When it gets dark, we'll move on for a mile. Let the ponies eat all they can while they are resting. We'll have to picket them when we go to sleep. Jed, it's your turn to prepare supper."

Jed built a fire from the dried oak twigs lying on the ground and with his ax broke up some larger pieces. He found some dried grass and spent some little time working it into a mass of dusty splinters. With his flint and steel he struck a spark in his tinder and soon fanned it into a flame. He got out the large frying pan and quickly made up a meal of salt pork and corn cakes. Hungrily the men devoured the food, their appetites making it taste extra good.

After cleaning up, Standage said to Jed, "Let's sit under this tree, Jed, and let me read to you what I was talking about this afternoon." Standage pointed to two books, the Bible and the Book of Mormon. "You put this Book of Mormon in your pack, and whenever you have time you read it. It will do you good, and you will understand us better then."

They read as much of the story as they could until darkness fell on the camp.

"Put out the fire, Jed," said Standage.

Jed carried water in the camp bucket and doused the red embers. The men silently and quietly brought in the horses. Each one saddled his own mount and helped saddle and arrange the packs on the pack animals. Then they all mounted, and with Standage in the lead and Cox bringing up the rear, they silently drifted away in the darkness.

After a half-hour of travel, Standage said, "I guess this will do." They were on a little ridge overlooking a small valley.

"We will go down in the valley where we will not be silhouetted against the sky."

Into the little depression they rode until Standage called a halt. Each man unsaddled his horse without talking, and attached long picket ropes to the horses' necks. Then taking the horses out about forty yards from where they were standing, each man drove a peg in the ground and tied his animal securely with about fifty feet of rope so it could move and feed.

One of the men was appointed to stand guard for half the night. The remainder sought their blankets, and soon quiet descended over the camp as tired men slept a well-earned sleep.

TEN

Sutter's Fort

THE LITTLE CAVALCADE OF MEN including Jed Colby wound its way along the banks and through the trees of the American River.

They had been told that Sutter was building a fort and a sawmill and was in need of men. The company of Mormon soldiers needed money to gain provisions to make the last long ride to the Rockies where they expected to meet their families. The news that they might obtain work was indeed welcome.

Now they were approaching the clearing which must be Sutter's Fort. There stood the log building freshly made, and a short distance away was a partly finished structure with a long ditch leading toward it.

They pulled up to the hitching rail, tied up their horses, and walked into the office of the fort. A tall, distinguished-looking man arose to meet them.

Standage put out his hand, "My name is Standage," he said. "I presume you are Mr. Sutter?"

"That's right," came the reply, "What can I do for you?"

"I understand that you are looking for men to help build your sawmill. We're heading east to the mountains, and we need some work to buy provisions. If you can give us work, we'll be glad to hire out to you."

"That I can, if you are good workmen. I'll hire you on one basis only," said Sutter. "If you work with me, you must agree to stay with me until the sawmill is finished and in operation."

"That we will," said Standage.

"Then it's a deal," said Sutter. "When will you start?"

"Soon as we can put our gear away. Where do you want us to go?"

"There is a bunkhouse behind this building," said Sutter. "You stay there."

Sutter supplied them with axes, shovels, saws, and planes, and showed them where to work. Soon they were sawing wood and hewing corners of logs to make tight joints for the building; some were digging in the millrace; and all were happy that they had found means to continue their journey.

Sutter employed a large crew of men to work on his mill, and it looked as if the mill would be finished within a month or two. One afternoon, after they had been working at it for about a month, Jed went to the mill office to draw provisions for the men. While he waited for Mr. Sutter to prepare the groceries, one of the men who had been working on the millrace entered. He had a wild gleam in his eye, and he carried in his hand a small buckskin sack.

"Could I have a word with you, Mr. Sutter?"

"Why, yes, Marshall."

With a dramatic gesture Marshall emptied his buckskin sack onto the counter. "What do you make of these, Mr. Sutter? It looks like gold to me. Can you tell gold?"

Sutter said, "It looks like gold to me, but I've seen fool's gold before, and I don't want to be deceived. Suppose we make a test."

He took a hammer and a flat piece of iron. He laid the piece of ore on the iron. With the hammer he struck several blows. The metal merely flattened out and got thinner the more he pounded.

"It's gold, all right," said Sutter. "Where did you find it?"

"I was digging dirt out of the millrace, and where the water had been running and washed all the loose mud out, in the clear gravel I saw this yellow gleam. I picked these pieces out of it."

"You could become rich, Marshall, and so could we all. Suppose you say nothing about it to the men until we find out how rich the finding is and where it came from."

"That's agreeable with me," said Marshall.

"We'll talk some more tomorrow," said Sutter.

But the word got out, and before morning the camp was ablaze with excitement. By noon not a man of the work crew remained with Sutter. All were busy packing to go out to pan gold.

Sutter was half wild with anger and anxiety. Men deserting their jobs meant that the mill would not be completed. The little group of battalion men sat quietly talking things over.

Said Browett: "Looks to me like here's our chance to strike it rich. Jackson panned out $100 yesterday. Soon as word leaks out there will be thousands here. And we're here first and can get the best claims." The logic of his words struck home. No one could answer that.

Standage slowly whittled a stick as his friends talked. Finally when it seemed that all would decide to pan gold, he had his say.

"You don't have to do what we've agreed to do," he said. "All of you are free men to do as ye like. When we came here, we agreed to stick by Sutter until the mill was finished. It's more than us, brethren; it's our people out yonder on the plains. We've somehow to show the world that they misjudged us. Sutter has influence. He's going to be here a long time. We're going to need him as a friend. I think we ought to stay by the mill till it's finished—and that's exactly what I aim to do. We can pan a little gold mornin' and evenin', and then when the mill's done we can give it a hard go for a couple of months before we start home. Besides, we promised we'd stick. That's as I see it."

"I think you're right," said Cox. "Let's stay and finish the mill."

And so it was voted.

Standage walked up to Sutter.

"Mr. Sutter, our boys are as anxious to stake claims and find gold as anyone else—maybe more so. We're here on the ground ahead of everyone else. But we Mormons like to keep our word. We gave our word we'd stay till the mill is finished. We'd like you to know we've decided to stick by you."

Sutter's face relaxed, and he smiled.

"Thank you, boys, for the favor. I'll not forget it."

The work on the sawmill was resumed. Standage led Jed into the woods among the giant trees. Never had he seen trees like these. They seemed to have no tops—up and up they towered until seemingly lost in the blue vault of heaven. Jed never forgot the experience of these months working in the woods felling trees. It was a long process—felling, peeling, notching, fitting, placing—but interesting. And Jed was under the direction of experts. These men knew how to fell trees. Raised in the east they were woodsmen all. Jed marveled at the way they worked.

Said Cox one day, "I'll lay this tree right on that spot." That spot was a direction opposite to the natural lean of the tree.

"I don't believe you can," challenged Jed.

So Cox went to work, cutting two notches at angles learned from long experience. The tree began to fall, but the control was with the axman, and when it crashed it was lying exactly as Cox had predicted. Jed envied his ability and practiced hard to duplicate it. He acquired some skill but couldn't fell a tree very close to where he intended it to fall.

All things have an end, and Sutter's mill was finally finished. The party quickly turned to panning gold. Cox had a good streak of luck and panned a considerable quantity. One evening Jed watched him cut into a piece of tanned buckskin.

"What you making?" he asked.

"A gold bag," replied Cox. "You see it works like this. I make a strong sack, then I sew to it a wide band of buckskin like this. That goes over my head and rests on my neck and shoulders. The bag hangs on my chest. Then I sew two strips to the bottom of the sack and tie them around my back—and there I have my gold as snug as a bug in a rug. No one gets the gold without getting me first. I have enough now to bring my wife and children to the valley—with good wagons and horses."

The next morning he said, "Standage, I've had enough panning gold. It's time for me to head east and meet my family. Suppose Dan Browett, David Allen, and I leave tomorrow ahead of the rest of you?"

"Suits me," said Standage. "Go ahead, and if you're not back in ten days, we'll know you got through the pass, and we'll start."

Cox and his friends gathered their supplies and equipment and by noon had disappeared in the great forest of the American River.

For ten days the remainder panned gold, gathered and repaired equipment, shoed horses, made ready. Finally Standage said, "Suppose we start in the morning."

And so the little party once more hit the long trail east. Their horses were fat and frisky from the long rest.

The trail led through groves of great trees. Occasionally they were forced to ford the rapid torrent of the river, sometimes they skirted great cliffs, and once they came out onto a ledge which overhung an immense drop of thousands of feet. And then the pass. Gradual had been the ascent on the west side, so they were not prepared for what they saw. The mountain fell steeply away to the east so that the whole panorama of the Great Basin met their eyes. Range upon range rose up out of this valley floor, the end of each terminating as suddenly as it had begun. One could almost pick out the trail east as it must go to dodge these immense ridges.

Toward night of their seventh day they arrived at a spring of water.

"Let's camp," ordered Standage. "No point in going farther till we've had supper."

"Look's like someone's been here before," said Johnson. The campground certainly was in great disorder. Scattered about were pieces of cloth, broken pack saddles, cooking pots, frying pans.

"Someone must have left in a hurry without time to pick up their belongings."

Jed wandered around the spot looking for something he could use. As he came into a place where the grass was thick, he noticed a brown object half hidden in the long grass.

"Standage," he called, "come here, quick!"

Standage rushed over to him.

"What is it?" he asked.

"Look here," and Jed stooped and picked up a brown buckskin bag. A loop for the neck had been cleanly cut, and the dangling strip bore the marks of a sharp knife.

"That's Cox's bag! But where's Cox? The gold's still in the bag! Boys, there's been foul play. Scatter and see what you can find!" Standage was sharp in his command.

A short distance to one side they found three partially filled holes. No one needed to imagine the truth that they feared. A shovel was brought and shortly they exposed to view the bodies of their three old friends. With tragic horror they pieced together what must have happened. Set upon suddenly by Indians as they made their camp, they had apparently had little chance to defend themselves. Cox, fearing the worst, had managed to cut loose his bag of gold and drop it in the grass before he had been struck on the head and killed. All the bodies were mutilated.

The next day, the men sadly dug three graves and gave proper burial to their friends. With axes they cut a headboard and carved the names of their slain comrades, with the date.

Henderson Cox
David Allen
Daniel Browett
July 1848

A sermon was preached, the graves dedicated. Then the little party faced the east, continuing the journey.

Standage took charge of the bag of gold. "I'll take this to Sister Cox," he said. "She'll be needing it more than ever now."

Epilogue

THE HORSES OF THE PARTY turned the point of the hill and headed for the squatty square fort in the valley of the Salt Lake. Off to the left steam seemed to arise from some warm pools or springs.

Already they had greeted several parties of men on horses heading north. Captain James Brown, their old battalion companion, had invited them to stay at Brown's Fort on the Ogden River, but Standage had told him about the gold for Mrs. Cox and pressed on.

"Well, boy," he said to Jed, "we're about there. I hope you're going to want to stay."

Jed was silent.

Curiosity spurred them to turn their horses over to the left to see the steaming pools. Standage dismounted by the side of one. He stopped and inserted his hand. "Just right," he said. "It's been a long time since I've had a bath. What do you say, Jed?"

Jed had a sudden surge of desire.

"Why can't I be baptized?" he suddenly said. "I believe all you've told me. I want to join you."

"If you believe, you may!" said Standage.

"Then let's do it now."

"Having been commissioned of Jesus Christ—," began Standage.

Jed felt a sweet peace. "I baptize you…" The water closed over his head. As they stepped from the water, Jed Colby had found a new life with his new friends.